THESE GAMER
SIBLINGS ARE
BADASSES—
AND THEY HATE
SELECTING A
"NEW GAME"

No Game
No Life

5

YUU KAMIYA

The soulless puppet had merely searched people's faces for hope, *praying*. Praying that somewhere out there someone might actually be *playing*. Hoping that, at the very least, the puppet show might be worth something to someone, he kept smiling.

Why would we be worried or afraid? —As long as our hands are touching. ——We're not gonna lose to anyone.

"...Brother, let's go—!"

"My full, unadulterated, unrestrained, unreserved power, 100 percent— Heavenly Smite— Here it is! ♥"

THE TEN COVENANTS

The absolute law of this world, created by the god Tet upon winning the throne of the One True God. Covenants that have forbidden all war among the intelligent Ixseeds—namely.

1. In this world, all bodily injury, war, and plunder is forbidden.
2. All conflicts shall be settled by victory and defeat in games.
3. Games shall be played for wagers that each agrees are of equal value.
4. Insofar as it does not conflict with "3," any game or wager is permitted.
5. The party challenged shall have the right to determine the game.
6. Wagers sworn by the Covenants are absolutely binding.
7. For conflicts between groups, an agent plenipotentiary shall be established.
8. If cheating is discovered in a game, it shall be counted as a loss.
9. The above shall be absolute and immutable rules, in the name of the God.

10. Let's all have fun together.

CONTENTS
05

YUU KAMIYA

NEW YORK

NO GAME NO LIFE, Volume 5
YUU KAMIYA

Translation by Daniel Komen
Cover art by Yuu Kamiya

NO GAME NO LIFE
©YUU KAMIYA 2013
First published in 2013 by
KADOKAWA CORPORATION,
Tokyo.
English translation rights reserved
by Yen Press, LLC under the license
from KADOKAWA CORPORATION,
Tokyo, through Tuttle-Mori Agency,
Inc., Tokyo.

English translation © 2016 by Yen
Press, LLC

Yen On
1290 Avenue of the Americas
New York, NY 10104

Visit us at yenpress.com
facebook.com/yenpress
twitter.com/yenpress
yenpress.tumblr.com
instagram.com/yenpress

First Yen On Edition: December 2016

Yen On is an imprint of Yen Press,
LLC.
The Yen On name and logo are
trademarks of Yen Press, LLC.

Library of Congress
Cataloging-in-Publication Data

Names: Kamiya, Yu, 1984– author,
    illustrator. | Komen, Daniel,
    translator.
Title: No game no life / Yuu Kamiya,
    translation by Daniel Komen.
Other titles: No gemu no raifu.
    English
Description: First Yen On edition. |
    New York, NY : Yen ON, 2015–
Identifiers: LCCN 2015041321 |
    ISBN 9780316383110 (v. 1 : pbk.) |
    ISBN 9780316385176 (v. 2 : pbk.) |
    ISBN 9780316385190 (v. 3 : pbk.) |
    ISBN 9780316385213 (v. 4 : pbk.) |
    ISBN 9780316385237 (v. 5 : pbk.)
Subjects: | BISAC: FICTION /
    Fantasy / General. | GSAFD:
    Fantasy fiction.
Classification: LCC PL832.A58645
    N6 2015 | DDC 895.63/6—dc23 LC
    record available at
    http://lccn.loc.gov/2015041321

ISBNs: 978-0-316-38523-7 (paperback)
    978-0-316-38524-4 (ebook)

10 9 8 7 6 5 4 3

LSC-C

Printed in the United States of
America

 NORMAL START

Welcome to a frontier where infinite possibilities await—now with over seven billion active users! Go forth and tell a story that no one but you can tell!

...Reality. Our precious lives, when you step back and look at them, are a kind of game. Try imagining the game described by the exciting copy above. A literal once-in-a-lifetime adventure—the grand game of life.

You start playing. First, there's a random character creation process that proceeds automatically as a collaboration between your parents. There's the heartwarming opening with your mom and your dad and a thousand blessings and all that, and then finally, you get to dive in. You get a rough grasp on the controls, and then you're tossed into "school," a microcosmic tutorial for the heavy seas of society—

The game's setting—Earth. Awaiting us as we're tossed into a corner of that oversized map is a massive sandbox game. There we have a vast array of choices, a spectacular degree of freedom, and count-less minigames. Inspired by the hype, we advance just as advertised, but it's not long before we realize something.

—We've been had.

Infinite possibilities—sure, that might be technically true. But the thing is, no one ever said you could do whatever you want in this game. Your level's not high enough; your stats are too low; you have insufficient funds; your start position cuts you off. Countless shack-les constrict the freedom the game boasted, making a mockery of it.

But—we say as we struggle. Believing the billing, we fall and fall and get up again, convinced that infinite possibilities and sparkling hope stretch out before us. And so we work hard to raise our levels, improve our stats, make money. Passive skills like "Talent" and "Capacity" were randomly assigned to us in character creation, and we grumble that it's not fair at all how some people have them and others don't. Never giving up, never giving in, grinding away for more experience points, struggling with all we've got—it's that kind of game.

The story sets your heart on fire. It's truly moving, isn't it?

—But it's meaningless.

No matter how high your score gets, you can never beat this game. Even once you've got the levels, the stats, the cash, everything—now they criticize you. Why?

—Because you "tried too hard." They tell you it isn't fair at all. Even though you won through your own effort. As soon as you have something other people don't, you're told it's cheating. And then you get penalized. You get handicapped with all kinds of abstract and concrete shackles imposed on you by the seven billion other play-ers. And then, at last, a certain suspicion likely flickers through your mind.

—Do you really have freedom in this game at all?

* * *

No matter what choices you make, society, other players—someone—steps in and edits them. You try to roll with it and go for the win again, but the same thing always happens. And then, all of a sudden, you look back at the road you've walked and can't help but see the truth: Your actions had nothing to do with your will. They were decided by someone else, directed, carried out under a tacit understanding. All there is behind you is a long path that they demanded you walk. That they—made you walk. In a flash, your suspicion turns to doubt with a shade of conviction. They were right: This bullshit game called life is indeed a vast, grand sandbox. But—you aren't the player.

Then you look down at your hands.

—When you see the countless strings entangling them, your skepticism turns to certainty. And then suddenly you look around.

—Seeing those same, innumerable strings ensnaring everyone else, your conviction becomes understanding. In heads clattering as they're shaken, the gamers realize that they themselves are mere puppets. That all they are in this game of life, where they'd taken the cues and played their parts, are puppets in a puppet show—NPCs.

Now, with all this in mind, I'd like to ask a question. *What is the purpose of your life?*

—Were you able to give an answer you're sure was your own?

—......

—This is the world that the empty puppet saw. In the ten years since the puppet had started the game, he had never questioned this fact. The soulless puppet had never mourned it, never bemoaned it. He'd merely searched people's faces for hope, *praying*. Praying that somewhere out there someone might actually be *playing*. Hoping that, at the very least, the puppet show might be worth something to someone, he kept smiling.

*   *   *

—Until that day.

███

Elven Gard—in the state of Tírnóg, the city of Loamigel. In the largest country in the world—its vast territory spanning three continents—among its fifty-two states, this was the capital of one. The capital was situated in the southeast, a metropolis that bordered Hardenfell, the country of Dwarf.

—A city of Elves, born of the forest and beloved by the forest. Loamigel's appearance was entirely different from that of the streets of Immanity—of Elkia. Over the center of the city towered the Bál Bél—an unspeakably vast tree that spread its foliage above the clouds and whose roots crawled through the ground like blood vessels to lay out the city's network of roads. The spaces between these roads were filled by houses and streetlamps, themselves formed from the intricate interweaving of trees and vines that sprouted from the earth. It bore only a superficial resemblance to "architecture"—the phenomenon of clearing forests, flattening the earth, and laying wood and stones on top of it. It was a living city, made possible by advanced magical engineering. In this landscape that united the urban and the natural stood a particularly large residence. It was the mansion of the state governor—Lord Ron Barthel. Through its rose-woven gates now passed a lone girl.

Blonde hair with soft curls. Long ears protruding, the sign of the Elf. On her forehead, a red gem caught the sunlight and sparkled gently. Greeting her was an aging man in fine garb with similarly long ears.

"Welcome, Miss Fiel. Or had I best address you as Lady Nirvalen?"

The girl named Fiel returned a fluffy, polite smile.

"Why, Lord Barthel, surely you may address me as you please. After all, I have not officially inherited the headship."

The man—Barthel—twisted his lips into a grin at her answer. He took a step back and extended his hand to invite Fiel into the mansion where all was woven of wood.

"It is most disgraceful of me to have forced a lady to wend her way from afar all the way to this provincial estate."

"Hee-hee, how *skillful* you are at uttering words utterly absent from your heart!"

"You wound me. Though I may be old, I mean to retain a heart capable of appreciating lovely flowers...though such flowers be unsightly weeds in my garden, you see?"

"Well, flowers of value choose for whom they would brightly bloom. And *when*, I might add."

Without dropping their smiles, but also without looking into each other's faces, the two walked. Barthel guided Fiel into the courtyard. At the center of the garden emblazed with all kinds of flowering plants stood a white-painted table and two chairs. As Fiel seated herself in one, Barthel settled into its opposite.

"It is then a trifle of a task for the both of us, I see. Shall we get started?"

They could come right to business.

"Regarding the coming election for the Upper House—Nirvalen, may I ask that you stand down as a candidate?"

Barthel addressed her by her family name alone as if giving an order.

—It had been Fiel who had given him leave to address her as he pleased—but there was an understanding among the nobles. Addressing one by family name alone was tantamount to an insult, but Fiel glowed back without batting an eye.

"Why, is *that* all?"

"Of course *not*. I would also require that you lend the name of Nirvalen officially to support my candidacy."

"Ahh, how *interesting*."

"Oh, and I would also appreciate it if you would take on the deposit for my candidacy, as well as my campaign fund. Additionally, my dear Lord Kastlet seems to have an interest in this 'Harp of Golden Dragon Bone' you possess. He has indicated that he might support me in the election if I could procure it."

"Oh *my*… Why, that is a precious heirloom of my *family*. It is said an entire *city* was granted in exchange—"

"So I hear. I am sure Lord Kastlet will be delighted."

Barthel grinned twistedly. He leered down at the ample bosom of the girl seated across from him.

"Ah, but I do not ask this immediately. For today, you are welcome to retire in the second house before returning. It seems to me it would be best for us to have a thorough conversation regarding future developments, perhaps through the night. Hmm?"

"Why, however you strive to put forward a refined appearance, your true self *never* changes." Fiel spoke as if about to burst into laughter. "Fundamentally, what you are saying is, 'Give me the status, give me the money, give me the lady,' is it not? Why, *these* days I suppose even the bandits of Immanity make demands with greater humility."

"Worms do know their place, after all. Do you not suppose that this bearing befits a man of my stature?"

"Why, not in the slightest, *Sir*, but you certainly are free to hold that opinion if you *wish*."

Fiel continued without breaking her gentle smile.

"And may I take it that you are making such *requests* of me as a consequence of a hangover?"

"Ha-ha-ha, I prefer the intoxication of flowers to that of spirits. Surely upon coming here, you must have anticipated that I might make such requests? After all…"

Barthel snapped his fingers. The spirit presence sharpened, and on the table appeared a steaming tea set. Subsequently, a slip of paper danced out to slide in front of Fiel.

"…You must be aware of the circumstances, in which an acting member of the Upper House is plotting to free the slaves— If you do not feel that this information becoming public would pose a problem, I certainly will not object if you refuse. Hm?"

Fiel maintained her composure despite Barthel's baiting. She merely ran her eyes over the slip of paper that had dropped on the table. What was documented there was simple: It was a list of records

and evidence of the maneuverings orchestrated by Fiel. Considering that Elven society could not function without the system of slavery, such acts were essentially criminal. Should this list become public, it would not be surprising if Fiel and any accomplices were charged with high treason—

"Given the scope of your knowledge, *Sir*, I must wonder why it is that you do not report this matter forthwith."

"I am a libertarian as well as an opportunist. What profit would there be for me in exposing your *gambit*?"

"And so you intend to blackmail me, do you? Why, I can only applaud the dexterity of your thought."

"'Blackmail'? Such a horrid word… I merely implore you, foolish maiden. Will you not come and accept my strict discipline, crawling on your hands and knees and wagging your rump? Hm?"

"If I may be so bold, Sir—may we proceed to the matter at hand?"

"Ah, you are beside yourself with excitement, hmm? Very well."

With this, Barthel snapped his fingers once more. Forthwith, a complex magical pattern glowed through the air, producing a deck of cards.

"Let us play oracle card—surely the rules need no explanation?"

Oracle card. A common, simple game among Elves, in which players competed using a hand of twenty-two cards and the extent of their magic.

—It was a dangerous game, primarily used in place of duels and disadvantageous to Fiel, who was the lesser mage. According to the Ten Covenants, Fiel, as the challenged party, had the right to determine the game—

"Why *certainly*, and let us clarify what it is we shall wager."

But Fiel batted not an eye, only responding carefully without looking away. The two would confirm their demands of each other—demands that would be absolutely binding under the Ten Covenants.

"Then I shall demand your person—and lifelong, all-encompassing submission."

"As for *us*, why, we demand that you *forget* about us, and that you assist us unconditionally and *unreservedly*."

—They were obvious stakes. If Barthel acquired Fiel's person, the entire house of Nirvalen along with her chastity would fall into his hands. Meanwhile, if Fiel prevailed, she would eliminate the basis for his blackmail while grasping the opportunity to wring him dry.

"Why, this all sounds quite fine, except—a petty villain such as yourself, my *lord*, had best not expect to win *everything*... Why, don't you know that when dexterity of thought reaches a certain point, it is called *delusion*?"

"How amusing your transparent bravado is, hmm? Do you suggest that the shame of Nirvalen stands a chance before me?"

Their gazes locked in challenge, and simultaneously, they declared:

""—*Aschente.*""

As if in anticipation of these words, the rite on the table activated, and the game began. Barthel and Fiel were each uniformly dealt a hand of twenty-two cards. The cards pinned themselves in the air, shuffling so that neither player could see the other's order. Then the two faced each other with hands of the same size and kind.

—This was oracle card. The simple game using the twenty-two cards of the tarot's Major Arcana deck commenced.

—Of the games played among Elves, this was one in which magical cheating was all but impossible. For, given that players can see the rite and the flow of magic, if magic were employed, it would be discovered immediately, constituting a loss. For this reason, it was popular among Elves to use self-operating magical items such as this deck. Among such games, oracle card was particularly favored, for its gameplay as well as its clear demarcation of victory—to be specific:

"—Two-card set."

At Fiel's brief whisper, two of the cards floating before her disappeared, instantaneously and silently reappearing facedown on the table. Barthel smiled, then announced:

"—Two-card set."

This time, two cards disappeared from Barthel's hand, and as before, they appeared on the table. Both having produced two cards from their respective hands, their contest was ready to begin. Barthel asked:

"So, are you ready?"

"Why, *yes*. With *that*—"

They both declared:

""—Open deal.""

At these words, all the cards they'd placed on the table flipped over at once. Suddenly—as if space was bursting—a vast spirit presence swelled. The cards Barthel had chosen were Strength and The Chariot. The scroll was Knight of Honor. Fiel's cards were The Fool and The Lovers. The scroll: Falling Down. Light poured forth from each of their melds, and before each of them arose a faint, translucent specter. Barthel had summoned a knight in full armor. The knight drew his sword, spurred on his horse, and charged. Before him, called out by Fiel's cards, tottered a half-nude maiden. The maiden, as if dancing, hung to the knight's neck, and she whispered something in his ear. The knight, as if in torment, raised his head—and turned his sword. Returning, holding the maiden, he rode toward his summoner, Barthel—to strike.

—Rank Seven, Elf, with the highest magical aptitude among the Ixseeds. The oracle cards they'd built were on the cutting edge of magical engineering. The fragmentary rite deployed by the composite seal of the cards attacked Barthel ruthlessly. Barthel, for his part—just clucked. He raised his hand and assembled a magical defense in an instant. Two magical circles floated up in the air and intercepted the sword of the onrushing knight. Light burst with a boom. The massive quantity of spirits scattered mowed over the garden as if licking it and dispersed. Barthel, having taken a harsh blowback, yet said placidly:

"To think you would use an attack-reversing scroll on the first turn. It gives the impression of an incompetent cowering before the threat of injury. Hm?"

To this, Fiel answered without interrupting her smile:

"Why, it is a *natural* hedge against risk in the first move. And it would hardly be amusing if the match were to end so *suddenly*."

"Ha-hmm, this is just what makes you so distressing to watch... To attempt such artifice in this game betrays a boundless lack of sense. I suppose I must educate you in the sort of behavior that suits my noble blood, hmm?"

So, to sum up, this was oracle card.

—A game for duels among Rank Seven, Elf. Both players held the same twenty-two-card hand and selected cards two at a time to form "scrolls." Each scroll, besides raw strength, had certain affinities, and the losing player would have to receive the attack that corresponded to the scroll. Defending against the attack relied on the player's magic. Used cards were discarded on the table, and, after eleven turns—that is, after all the cards had been used—the player had to choose whether to resign or to continue. If the game continued, then each player would start the contest with twenty-two cards once more—and so on until one player could hold out no longer. There were 231 scrolls in total—it was impossible to predict and prepare for all of them. Therefore, victory depended on the ability to continue defending against attacks.

—In short, it was a test of one's ability as an Elven mage. "Quadcasters" were considered the best of the best. Barthel was not quite up to that level, but still a remarkable mage as a "tricaster." Fiel, meanwhile—

"—You rely on link tattoos and boosters for beginners just to achieve duocasting, and you sincerely believe you can defeat me, do you—shame of Nirvalen, hm?"

—Indeed. The decisive factor for victory in this game was magic skill. The number of rites that could be deployed concurrently—also implied the power and frequency of magic that could be applied. Against a tricaster such as Barthel, Fiel, barely a duocaster, didn't stand a chance. But Fiel laughed it off.

"Why, of *course* I do. You're making *quite* the show over having blocked only my first move, but why not wait to crow until you actually land an *attack*?"

Then, she glanced upward. From the garden where the flowers danced and scattered in the still-throbbing spirits, she could see the second floor. Through the window, she saw walking a black-haired, black-clad girl—her partner—and her face softened. Yes, this game properly had no place for an Immanity, bereft of magic, to get involved. A single blow would be enough to decide the matter. It could hardly even be called a game. *But*—two faces flashed through Fiel's mind. Self-assured, sarcastic, yet somehow melancholy, a man and a girl whispered.

—*Who said you had to take them head-on?*

And so—

"Why, this game was over before it began!"

■■■

"...*Tsk*, damn that Barthel."

On the second floor, Fritz, a butler of the house of Barthel, clucked with bile at the match in the garden.

—His master's intent was clear to see from the covenant he had set out. He would seize upon her weakness, goad her into an unwinnable game, and take possession of her person. Once he defeated the girl, he would automatically own the Nirvalen family's votes, interests, property, and—more important than anything, more valuable than gold—those tits. You could see he'd put on his smug bad-guy face, but it could be assumed that his mind had already left the game behind and moved on to later that night in bed and tits galore. Fritz knew this because, as he blocked the card attacks on Barthel's behalf from where the girl couldn't see—in other words, helping Barthel cheat—his own mind was full of tits galore.

Shame of Nirvalen? Incompetent? What did it matter? Those tits were enough to wipe all other defects clean from the slate. A woman, after all, was about her knockers. If those knockers were complemented by a nice face, fine buttocks, curvaceous hips, and long legs, that was all well and good, but everything beyond the knockers was optional and had about as much value as the paper napkin that comes with your lunch.

Intelligence? Magic? Such trifles were of no interest whatsoever.

—To get straight to the point, Fiel pushed Fritz's buttons *hard.*

"Oh, fancy seeing you here. You are Lord Barthel's butler... Fritz, was it?"

"—?! You're Nirvalen's—"

As the manservant spun about in a panic, there stood a black-haired, black-clad Immanity...Nirvalen's slave. *Chlammy, was it?* Fritz clucked to himself.

"...*Tsk*, you flat-chested wench. Mind your manners before you speak to me."

To begin with, being addressed by such a pathetically endowed Immanity was obnoxious. And now, of all times, was inopportune. He was laden with the duty of supporting Barthel while appreciating every last bit of Fiel's tits. But, as if incapable of discerning what ran through Fritz's mind, the flat-chested wench continued amiably:

"Fate must have brought us together here. Why don't you *challenge* me to a game?"

"...Watch your tongue, you kept bitch. You'd best at least triple the size of your breasts before opening your mouth, you inferior *thing.*"

The words resounded with contempt, derision, and countless ill intentions.

Yet the girl merely replied, "Watch my tongue...you say? For instance—"

Still smiling, she narrowed her eyes.

"If I were to use it to expose the misconduct of Lord Barthel and yourself—what would you think of that?"

"...What's this about?"

"You are thinking that an Immanity is incapable of detecting magic—I suppose?"

"......"

As he fell silent, the flat-chested girl shook her head theatrically. "You would be right. Hypothetically. Just *hypothetically*, mind you. For a duocaster to win against a tricaster, it would be difficult, but not impossible. However, if you were to conspire with Lord Barthel and help him block her card attacks from here, your game would result in almost certain victory. Meanwhile, I, being unable to detect magic, would be unable to prove such shenanigans. My master—Fi—would be in quite a bind, wouldn't she?"

"……"

But— The flat-chested girl broke into a giggle as she continued.

"There's no need for me to detect it, you know? After all, *you will confess*."

"…What?"

"I'll say this one more time: Why don't *you* challenge me to a game? If you refuse—" The girl flashed a dusky smile and produced a small jewel from her breast pocket. "I shall let Public Safety know about your using Lord Barthel's funds to produce and sell these 'seeds' to the Dwarves—a neighboring country—so that you may savor your own ruin. Is that a better way to use my tongue?"

"Wha—?!"

Fritz loosed a groan. Of course, the small stone Chlammy played with in her palm was none other than the "seed" in which he was dealing—illegal contraband.

"By concentrating spirits in liquid form and ingesting them, it is possible to boost the spirits within one's own body. It serves as a doping agent for magic. However, there are side effects—in fact, to such an extent that it became prohibited due to rampant abuse."

—In other words…

"A feeling of pleasure and omnipotence induced by overdose. That's what you call a drug."

"…!"

"Do you understand now? Challenge me. There is no other way for you to save yourself."

At Chlammy's chilly smile, Fritz pursed his lips. It was over. This was the end of the line.

"...Ngk!"

No—bear it. It's wasn't time; it was still too early to laugh...! It would be unsightly to break into a belly laugh at this flat-chested bint who *thought she had him cornered with information such as this*! Turning his face from the flat-chest, Fritz shook his shoulders weakly. Did it look like the fear of a cornered man? —How foolish. How terribly foolish. It was Barthel who had put Nirvalen up to this. In exchange for overlooking the information that Nirvalen was plotting to free the slaves, he'd forced her to accept a game under disadvantageous conditions. To make his victory certain, he'd tasked Fritz with assisting him. *But*—Fritz recalled the words of that super-bosom.

—And it would hardly be amusing if the match were to end so *suddenly...*

—*Those two... They were never going after Barthel in the first place, but me.* He stifled his laughter. Fiel's easy acceptance of Barthel's game was all planned. If Fritz had his hands full supporting Barthel, even a lone Immanity girl could corner him. *That kind of basic calculation* was transparent. To begin with, he'd *known this would happen.* He knew that his seed smuggling had been found out. He'd been informed in advance by Barthel himself that there would be an interruption during the game. The reason being that these two had brought the discussion to Barthel first.

—*Your butler is engaged in this criminal affair. We would like to force him to confess in secret so as not to damage your reputation as his master. We request your cooperation so that we can obtain information.*

And so they'd worked to set him up. The game unfolding in the courtyard had been fixed in advance with Barthel for that very purpose—

(...*Or so they think*— How ludicrous!)

The two hadn't realized that it was Barthel himself who was actually the ringleader—Barthel, the very one who'd asked them to help. Barthel couldn't take out Fritz. If Fritz confessed, not only the smuggling routes but also a mountain of evidence indicating the true ringleader would come out. Therefore, Barthel had pretended to collaborate with them, only to bring Fiel into his grasp. He had proposed the idea himself and chosen his own mansion as the stage. Given the assumption that this was secret, she could have no allies here but her flat-chested slave.

—What a farce. A pathetically endowed Immanity and a pathetically stupid rack. They thought they were setting him up as they leaped right into the spider's web.

"...You are stupider than I thought. Let me explain this in a way that even an idiot can understand."

As Fritz stifled his laughter, the flat-chest spoke as if throwing cold water on him.

"You do not have any choice. It's play or be smashed. You get it?"

Spluttering at the comical taunt, Fritz raised his head. He removed his eyes from the courtyard and fixed them on the girl before him. Maintaining his composure with all his might, Fritz seated himself at an adjacent table.

"...Very well. But I am a busy man. Let us make it quick."

"How convenient. I cannot afford leisure myself, given my partner's circumstances. We'll make it simple."

The flat-chest sat at the table after him and commenced.

"Here I have a perfectly ordinary deck of playing cards."

She drew three cards from the deck and laid them on the table. They were the ace, queen, and king of spades.

"King beats queen, ace beats king, and queen beats ace."

With that, she laid the three cards facedown and shuffled them.

"Each of us will draw one card facedown, and we will reveal them to decide the winner. Understandable enough for an idiot?"

"—Heh! And your request?"

"Are you not the one who should be making requests? Or pleas to spare your life, I might say," the flat-chest sneered.

Slightly irked, Fritz responded, "...Then I request the destruction and oblivion of all information you wenches have grasped regarding the smuggling."

"Yes, and I request your confession and testimony regarding all of it. Everything, you understand."

At these vague words, Fritz's brow twitched slightly. Her objective was—all the information about the smuggling and a confession about the cheating in the game proceeding in the courtyard. How interesting: These pathetic, stupid wenches, in their own stupid way, meant to stand here in consideration of their own interests. Little do they know, they came too late from the start...

"—Very well. *Aschente*."

"Yes, *Aschente*..."

—They drew their cards. His card still facedown, Fritz wove a little spell. *Did you think that, if I was assisting Barthel, I would be unable to use magic here?* Still the adversary was the shame of Nirvalen. Fiel Nirvalen—the first incompetent in the history of the house. She'd flunked out of school—the Garden—and was barely capable of even monocasting without the link tattoos and boosters on the back of her hand and forehead and so on. This trash was facing Barthel, a tricaster. Moreover, the foolish pair of tits was expecting the match to be thrown. What could come of Fritz diverting his attention for a mere moment?

—He looked through his facedown card. It was the ace. He'd unfortunately been unable to figure that out from the start, but this was a game proposed by his opponent. There was no question she was cheating. There was no magic present—this he could say for sure. Then how could an Immanity cheat—? She could have shuffled deliberately and controlled the cards they drew. In any case, it was certain that the flat-chest's card was the one that could beat his—the queen. Only three cards, presented from the beginning. Even if he were to repaint his facedown card from ace to king, his iniquity would be exposed as soon as the third card was overturned. But then all he had to do was to use magic to switch the faces of his card and hers. Even if she had drawn deliberately to acquire the card before her, that itself was cheating. And without the ability to detect magic, there was no way for an Immanity to prove that he had switched them.

—*Is that what you expect? I would advise you not to underestimate me, puny Immanity.* Silently, he touched his finger to the table. Instantly, the spirits that ran along the table told him the flat-chest's card: It was the king, which meant she'd assumed that he'd switch the facedown cards—and drew the losing card intentionally. Such a cheap trap. She thought using one of the oldest tricks in the book made her a tactician.

"—What can be expected of the shame of Nirvalen and her slave... Fools."

By this point, Fritz wasn't even trying to contain it. He laughed out loud.

"A foolish pair of melons being preferable to a clever flat-chest, a woman is most valuable if her nutrients go to her bosom rather than her brain— But when it comes to a foolish flat-chest, what can one even say?"

"...It appears they were right when they said noble character is not something one is born with."

The flat-chest twisted her face peevishly. Fritz swallowed quietly. There was nothing he had to do. She just had to fall into her own trap.

"Well then, open deal, all right?"

"Yes, and therein lies your downfall."

They revealed their cards simultaneously. Fritz's card, just as he had seen, was the ace. And the flat-chest's—

—was the *queen*.

"...H-how—?! It can't be!!"

Kicking away his chair as he stood, Fritz shrieked. Absurd, impossible, it wasn't— Fritz panted, but Chlammy smiled.

—Softly. Yes. *With a full-faced glow, as of the sun:*

"...Hee-hee, did it surprise you *it was not what you saw when you peeked?*"

—Chlammy's visage, along with her speech, swayed.

"When you use *magic*, why, you'd best look carefully at your *opponent* first?"

The visage of the black-haired girl evaporated like a summer haze, leaving a girl of waving blonde tresses—that is—

"Wench...you're Nirvalen?!"

Having *mimicked the visage of Chlammy*, she transformed back into *Fiel*.

"Why, *yes*, I am Fiel Nirvalen."

Fiel's lips curved in an arc, producing her fluffy smile.

"You were speaking of nutrients going to the bosom rather than the brain, I recall...? Why, this poses a rather interesting question. Wherever are your nutrients going—as it appears that even your *dear member* lacks development?"

Uncovering in an instant the details of Fritz's body by making spirits crawl over him, Fiel narrowed her eyes.

"Why, I can only weep for the sad nutrients you've ingested, only to put them to no use, whether above or below."

But Fritz had no attention to spare for such jests— He'd lost? To Nirvalen?!

"Why, there's no need for such *alarm*. It may be short and small, but I'm sure there are some who prefer it that way... Though when your brains and face are lacking as well, it's hard to make promises!"

—Then— Then what, then what, then what?!

"...Impossible! Then what of the one dueling Lord Barthel—? Who is she?!"

■■■

"*Chlammy*—why, I'm all done here."

Fiel Nirvalen leaned over the terrace railing and waved into the courtyard. That moment—the Fiel Nirvalen who was playing a game before her— No. *The girl who bore that appearance* returned to her original form as if casting off a veil. Chlammy Zell—the black-haired, black-clad girl revealed there—bowed gracefully.

"—Your cooperation is appreciated, Lord Barthel."

"...W-well. Of course I must bear responsibility for failing to identify indiscretions within my own ranks, hm."

At the Immanity girl lowering her head deeply to him, Barthel hid his discomfiture and furrowed his brow.

"B-but isn't this different from what we agreed upon? Hm? I understood you as promising to conduct this matter in secret... There was no mention of another participant."

At his words, the girl gave him a quizzical "I'm sorry?"

"Please excuse my impertinence, but, were there an uninvited guest in your mansion, would you not be the first to observe this, my lord?"

"...Mm-mmg..."

Indeed. Barthel closed his mouth. The only ones in the mansion were himself, Fritz, Fiel, Chlammy, and a few additional servants. It was his own house. Were there an intruder, he should be able to detect it immediately. He had cast a rite for that very purpose. Indeed, he had selected the location for the game with that in mind—yet. In that case, how had this Immanity girl been able to duel him? The black-haired girl beamed.

"Just as promised, we are alone, my lord."

"I-I see. Do excuse me... S-so now we can conclude this game as null and void, hm?"

—It was odd. Something was odd. Spurred by an unease that threatened to crush him, Barthel stood. For now, his highest priority was to brush off this game and figure out what to do next—

"What's this? It appears you are confused, Lord Barthel."

—At the freezing touch of these words, Barthel turned back. There sat Chlammy, a black-haired girl, wearing a grand sneer.

"Two-card set." Two cards vanished her from her hand and appeared on the table. "I'd remind you that our game is certainly not concluded."

"—Wha…?!" It was impossible to conclude the game without mutual consent. "W-wench, what are you plotting?!"

"To continue the game, of course. Please be seated. Though, if you fold, I will help myself to your chips."

At Chlammy's words, Barthel's eyes bulged. He had hardly listened to his opponent's demand, assuming that his victory was a fait accompli.

—That you forget about us, and that you assist us unconditionally and unreservedly.

Though the wording might have been different, the demand was the same as the one Barthel had made to Fiel—no, even greater. He would even forget that he had lost the game as he was reduced to their slave. While Barthel's demand had been this:

—Your person—and lifelong, all-encompassing submission.

In fact, the one who had accepted the game was not Fiel, but Chlammy. Winning would only gain him one slave of Nirvalen, a prize hardly worth taking. He'd meant to force through conditions that favored him—but instead had swallowed conditions that favored *her*—?!

"Y-you wenches—!"

"Lord Barthel? Your time is almost up. Do you mean to resign?"

His rage was countered by Chlammy's cool demeanor.

—A player who did not produce a card within the set time would automatically forfeit the match. Having just remembered that rule, Barthel shouted at his cards in a flurry.

"—! Two-card set!"

Obeying Barthel's shriek, two cards disappeared from his hand and appeared on the table. Chlammy turned up the corners of her mouth in a grin and said:

"Open deal."

With this declaration, the four cards on the table flipped over. Barthel's cards were The Moon and The High Priestess. The scroll was Double Shadow. Chlammy's cards were Justice and The Emperor.

The scroll was I Am the Rulebook. Barthel's scroll: one that dodged the opponent's attacks and spun them against the prosecutor. Chlammy's scroll: one that pressed through by its own will regardless of any status effects. The scrolls activated. The sword drawn by the Emperor lay bare the truth of the High Priestess and pulled her down off her perch. Having stripped his opponent of her might and authority, the Emperor's force rushed on toward the vacant Barthel.

"——Ngk?!"

He rushed to spin defense magic. Three spells activated just before the Emperor's sword would have struck. But the hastily erected guard creaked, and a burning load was placed upon Barthel's spirit corridor junction nerves. There was a boom and a flash, and a voice came from behind the breathless Barthel.

"Oh *my*. Why, it would *appear* that was sufficient to shave off half your strength!"

He turned to see Fiel calmly advancing with his crestfallen butler in tow.

"Fritz—you knave. How could you lose to Nirvalen?!"

Fritz winced at Barthel's censure, casting his gaze down wordlessly. Beside him, Fiel spoke with her fluffy smile.

"Why, what can you expect? Ultimately, he took me for an Immanity and let his guard entirely down."

"Shut your mouth, Nirvalen! You treacherous vixen, you deceived me?!"

"Whaaat? The word *deceive* is so offensive… Why, after all…"

Fiel looked at Chlammy, still seated at the table. Chlammy nodded and smiled coldly.

"…Weren't *you* the one who was always trying to put one over on *us*?"

Barthel gasped, but Chlammy continued.

"You were the one telling your butler to manage the smuggling so you could profit. Did you think we wouldn't realize?"

"Why, you thought you'd pretend to help, trap us, wipe out the evidence, and then take *everything*—"

"And if it didn't work out, you'd just annul the game and moon us... Rather deplorable, my dear lord."

At Fiel and Chlammy's invective, Barthel's face warped violently. They knew everything. They knew what he'd been plotting, and he was the one who'd been led by the nose... No.

"Heh, heh-heh... You missed your chance, Nirvalen!"

"Excuuse me? Did you call?"

As Fiel stared at him blankly, Barthel shrieked in triumph.

"Now that I know the one who was playing with me was this little hussy, it is transparent that you cheated! An Immanity could never guard against a card attack! You were helping her, weren't you?!"

—Indeed, since the start of the game, they had gone through three full decks, and seven battles further. Which meant that, in the course of forty rounds, Chlammy had received some attacks. Barthel had seen with his own eyes that they had been blocked by magical barriers. Chlammy couldn't have done this, and therefore Fiel must have helped her—*but*. The condemned Fiel scratched her cheek incredulously and grinned back.

"Why, considering that you were relying on your *butler*, this is a most *shocking* accusation..."

And then Chlammy told him.

"In the first place, that's not cheating—*you ass*."

The direct insult left Barthel speechless.

"Listen carefully to the words of a covenant you make—when you and I confirmed the conditions, I explicitly said *we*."

—Now Barthel truly had no more words. He merely opened his eyes. Given that she'd said *we*, it was considered a game between Barthel and the team of Chlammy and Fiel. There wasn't a rule against leaving one's seat during the game; Fiel could cast a barrier from a remote location without cheating— No, wait...*she'd been disguising both of them, hiding it from us, playing a game on the second floor, and at the same time casting a barrier—?*

With a sigh, Chlammy twisted her lips.

"Fi, it looks like this twit finally gets it."

"Well, you must consider that he is handicapped by all the blood flow going to his *loins* rather than his brain. Why not give him the credit he *deserves*?" Fiel spoke sunnily, but in a tone that conveyed nothing but cold. "Yet he falls so easily for such simple word games. It's disappointing. After preparing so many complicated tricks and backup plans—look, it's all gone to waste."

Before his eyes, a girl of an inferior race sighed as if disgusted with him.

"Anyway... Your play is so obvious. You always make a brute-force attack at the start. It gets blocked, and then you try a curse. You don't use counters because you don't like them, and just now you allowed your fear to take over, stalling for time with scrolls that annul attacks. Any bloody dunce could— Excuse me. Given this, it is hardly surprising that you do not understand."

Barthel's shoulders quivered. In rage and humiliation—and, most unspeakably, in *fear*. Throughout these forty rounds, Chlammy had suffered injury in only a scant few. And those had all been starting rounds, the ones in which luck played the biggest factor. For the rest—*she'd read every play he'd made.* Not an Elf, but a mere human, an Immanity—

"—Don't underestimate humans like that, you old creep."

The mysterious black-haired girl—

"...Come—let the game continue!"

—smiled at him like the Grim Reaper.

——......

The sharp spirit surge caught Barthel by the arm—and ripped at his spirit corridor junction nerves. At the ineffable agony, the old man of hundreds of years wailed like a child. After the shock that scattered the flowers that bloomed in the garden subsided—to the old Elf, fallen from his chair, grasping in torment, the Immanity girl whispered sweetly.

"—This marks the end of the fourth cycle. What seems to be the matter, Lord Barthel?"

"Eeegh—ee..."

"By the way, I wonder if you've noticed. Fi...that is, Fiel Nirvalen—is a hexcaster."

At these words poured into his ear, the old man's face blanched whiter than paper. He knew by now that this was no lie. It was the only explanation for the series of feats Fiel had pulled off that day. As if to console the pale, shivering old man, Chlammy knelt and continued.

"Fear not, my lord. I see you have no strength left to weave further barriers—but you still have ample chance of victory. All you have to do is read my every move without taking a single attack and wear down our hexcaster."

—Describing chances that would require scientific notation to express mathematically, Chlammy smiled.

"And it's no problem if you fail. It will only hurt a little—though you might die accidently."

—Indeed, what she'd described—*was exactly what she'd pulled off. Surely you don't mean to say that a mere human can do it and you can't—?*

"I— I-I— I concede! It is my loss! So please—please spare me!!"

"—Very well. Then we win, I see. Thank you for the match, Lord Barthel."

As Chlammy stood with a look askance at the pitiful old man, Fiel bounded upon her with a cheer.

"Why, how *wonderful*! This must be the first time an Immanity has ever defeated an Elf at *oracle card*!"

"…It's nothing worthy of boast against a senile buffoon such as this. He's the lowest of the low among *all the trash we've been playing.*"

Stroking Chlammy's swollen head comfortingly, Fiel turned with a *Well then*. She teased the splayed Barthel and Fritz, standing by his side, with her eyes.

"Shall we, Lord Barthel? By the Covenants, please forget *every-thing* about us."

And then—Chlammy continued with a smile.

"Carry on with your illegal trade as you were."

—Wha…what?

"And also, Mr. Fritz? Why, *half a month from now*—you will confess everything."

—What…in blazes?

As both Barthel and Fritz seemed woefully incapable of keeping up with what was transpiring, Chlammy stepped up to the table once more.

"With that, we shall presently be taking our leave—but first." She smirked while shuffling the tarot cards they had used for the game. "As a final courtesy, I will tell your fortune."

"Why, *Chlammy*, it is news to me that you had such a skill!"

"Indeed, this will be my first time. However—this fortune will not fail."

Her words were at once jocular and eerie as she drew four cards—

"Oh my, what interesting cards. Let's see, by my reckoning…"

On cue, she revealed each card in turn to her audience.

—Temperance, upright.

"It appears your business of selling seeds to the Dwarves will proceed quite smoothly."

—The Tower, upright.

"But then in half a month…goodness me, *for some reason*, one of your Dwarven customers will confess and get caught."

—Wheel of Fortune, reversed.

"And then, *unfortunately*, Lord Barthel, your butler will mention your name, and the whole affair will be traced back to you…and then."

—Judgment, reversed.

"You yourself, Lord Barthel, will be judged in a court of law—the end. My condolences."

Ignoring the blanching pair, Chlammy threw a theatrical question at Fiel.

"Heh-heh, that's rather interesting, isn't it, Fi? When Lord Barthel gets caught, whoever shall take ownership of that trading company of his, Will Andmorrow, the greatest in Elven Gard?"

"Oh *my*. Why, what a coincidence—it happens to be that boy of the house of Enrich we *amused ourselves with* three days ago."

—Everything. Everything had been in the palms of their hands. The two girls darkly laughed at what they called *destiny*.

"Nirvalen. You bitch—no, you bitches, just what are you plotting?!"

To Barthel, howling as his teeth chattered, the two responded with cold smiles.

"What's that? Well, we could tell you, I suppose."

"But you'll forget anyway. Much as you'll forget *you were involved with us at all*."

Watching the two witches giggle innocently to each other, Barthel shivered. *Just what had he got himself into?*

"Well then, by the Covenants—farewell, Lord Barthel."

"Why, we pray for your continued success in your business."

—And so. With a snap of the ladies' fingers, the day ceased to have been.

■■■

Chlammy and Fiel drew their matching hoods down over their faces. They weren't here, and they never had been. That's how it became. Hiding from view, they leaped from the top floor of Lord Barthel's mansion. Faster than gravity, the rite Fiel wove took hold of their bodies and carried them high in the sky.

—Through the wind, into the night. Only the red moon, the light of the stars, and the lamps of the city lit the scenery below them, brilliantly. A city in the forest. A city of green woven of astonishingly refined magic. It was a sight with which Chlammy was quite familiar—but, even if it had been the first time she was seeing it, it would have been indication enough that Elven Gard's civilization was on another level entirely. The two flitted through the sky above, their hoods flapping.

"Chlammy, why, you were amazing." From tree—no, from building to building, bounding roof to roof, Fiel gushed.

"You really took out that old scoundrel without my aid. Goodness, I was so concerned."

"...Never mind that, Fi. Are *you* all right?"

"Eh-heh-heh, it's not a bad feeling to have you concerned about me. You certainly are growing, Chlammy," Fiel responded with a silly smile while maintaining the rite allowing them to glide through the air. But the gem in her forehead had lost its sparkle and appeared cloudy due to her profligate use of magic. Chlammy could see this clearly, even in the dim light.

Lord Ron Barthel and his butler, Fritz. A tricaster and a duocaster. They might not have been the best of the best, but they were up there.

...*But*, Chlammy pondered, with a glance at the girl dancing through the air beside her.

—Fiel Nirvalen. The head of one of the few truly great families of Elven Gard, which Chlammy served as a slave. Fiel had attended the towering white tree of the greatest magic school in the nation, the Garden—and failed and withdrawn. Those who did not know her, with her white link tattoos and beginner boosters, sneered. She was the first incompetent since the birth of the house of Nirvalen—scrap, they said. But Chlammy, who knew Fiel was only feigning incompetence, sneered at the sneerers. Fiel was the greatest talent since the inception of the house of Nirvalen—gold—this she knew. Fiel had never particularly made a show of her true ability to Chlammy. But still—

She'd cast a spell of disguise on herself and Chlammy, and she'd cast a spell of blocked awareness both on Barthel and on Fritz to prevent them from catching on. On top of that, she'd defended Chlammy in oracle card from a distance, and what's more, she'd taken on Fritz in *their* game... She had been orchestrating *six spells at once*.

A hexcaster—without a doubt, she was better than the best.

No, wait. In that game with Sora and Shiro a while back—the Othello match using Jibril's core—Fiel had woven a rite capable of controlling the astronomical power wielded by Rank Six, Flügel.

Taking this into account, it was enough to imagine that she was a mage for whom "better than the best" didn't even cut it. A mage to be welcomed as an honorary instructor, even by the same Garden that had expelled her.

...It was very least they could do.

"Mmrr...? Why, what's the matter, Chlammy?"

With her golden locks fluttering in the wind and her white skin glowing in the darkness, Fiel's smiling form was more dazzling than the light of the sun. She was the flower of Nirvalen, born to a pedigreed house and concealing extraordinary intellectual and magical talent. Wherever she walked, a future of nothing but sparkles should have been her due—had she not herself thrown it all away. Yes, she had refused that promised future. Concealing her nature, playing the incompetent, she had chosen, of all things, to bite back at her homeland, her country, her race. All for one person. Just one. None other than—

"—...It is nothing."

—For her friend. Softly dropping her eyes, Chlammy exhaled. To free the slaves— Certainly, it had a nice ring to it. But it was tantamount to freeing the national secrets of Elven Gard. To free the Fairies, for instance, who'd been exploited for high-level magic, was equivalent to selling their secret weaponry to another country. If that happened, the Dwarves of Hardenfell could hardly pass up the chance. Elf would most likely lose the continent they'd been quarreling with Dwarf over for nearly a millennium. In the worst case, they'd go on to see their country split, and what lay at the end of that did not bear discussion.

—But if it was for Chlammy, Fiel's homeland could go to ruin for all she cared. So she boasted and so she truly thought, and in fact, she had already taken any number of perilous steps to that end. Toward Fiel, Chlammy felt deep gratitude as well as a certain feeling akin to admiration, which transcended race and age.

—But then what about herself? Chlammy had to wonder. Though it might not have shown on her face, Fiel's deep fatigue was evident in the color of her gem. As someone who couldn't win a single game without placing such a burden on one of Fiel's class...was she really worthy of being called a friend—?

—*Grk.* Her head throbbed. It was a flashback, Chlammy realized, as she stopped, holding her head in her hands.

—A girl and a puppet that wanted to be a person, joining pinkies and exchanging a promise. He—the puppet—Sora. Did he think that he would tie her down? Tether her to the ground, one who should have been free to ascend unaided to the heavens—

"Why...Chlammy, *whatever* is it?"

Chlammy replied, averting her eyes from the friend who'd doubled back after noticing she'd stopped. "...Fi, I'm sorry. If I'd only moved more skillfully..."

"Chlammy...?"

Elven Gard. It was an enormous country that wielded its overwhelming magical supremacy over almost 30 percent of the planet's landmass. It was the greatest nation in the world, with over twice the might of its closest competitor, Hardenfell. Its foundations were like a fortress, defying attempts to find a crack—

...No. That was just another excuse. Still thinking of those two, Chlammy tightened her fists.

"If they had been the ones playing—they could have done it without magic."

"Chlammy..."

Gradually, she and Fiel chipped away at those who held the reins of distribution, trade, and rights. Undercutting power beneath a veil of secrecy, at the end a tiny ant tunnel, a hole thinner than a needle opened. But, at this rate, they could never—

"And never mind that, they could have won more grandly!"

The more little games they stacked, the more catastrophe loomed. If the powers that be ever caught on to their machinations, they would be squashed in a blink. Somewhere, there had to be a Sora-style solution—to end it all with a single, unexpected strike.

"And yet...all I do is cause trouble for you, and we make no progress worth—"

"Chlammy!"

As the skin of her palms began to split, pierced by her fingernails in her clenched fists, a quiet but authoritative voice stopped her.

"Chlammy, why...you can't be them."

"......I know."

She looked down. She knew. It was futile, even if she tried to imitate Sora. It was Sora and Shiro together that made " " (Blank)— Immanity's greatest gamer. She would have to find her own—

"Why, no. You understand nothing, I'm afraid."

Her thoughts interrupted, Chlammy looked up.

"I don't know what sort of memories you received from Mr. Sora. But I do purport to know a bit—about who Mr. Sora *is*." In that forest city, amidst its fantastic illumination, Fiel's expression turned serious. "Why, Mr. Sora used you because he couldn't do it himself."

"...Fair enough, but look at—"

"And he used me because *you* couldn't do it yourself."

"—!"

"They are not the only one who is two. To begin with, attempting to win that game without relying on me would be as like unto Mr. Sora or Miss Shiro playing *alone*."

"...Fi..."

"*Chlammy*, why, you can rely on me. And you ought to."

Just as " " was a team, Chlammy and Fiel were, too. If they were able to produce the same results together, then to whom must they apologize? But—

"But all I do is weigh you down. I haven't—"

"Why, it's because of you that I have the will...and also..."

Holding her disheartened friend's hand, Fiel glowed.

"I'm perfectly aware, you know, of how every day you summon up those memories from Mr. Sora and try to uncover all of Mr. Sora and Miss Shiro's strategies to make them your own—"

Her eyes suddenly clouded with a somber tinge.

"And because of that, you haven't slept in forever."

"......"

"If you don't sleep, I won't sleep. If you will try, then I will try. Why, if you think *I* am tired—don't you see you are the same?"

With these words, Fiel peered into Chlammy's face.

—Stroking the dark circles even the night couldn't conceal, she whispered like a mother chiding her child:

"Chlammy, if you would worry about my fatigue, tonight is the night you must promise me you will sleep properly... Why, if we carry on like this, we'll both collapse..."

"...I'm sorry. I shouldn't have—"

"Mmng, why, that's not it." Fiel pouted comically, her cheeks puffed out. "Don't you think there's something else you should be saying?"

"...—You're right. Thank you, Fi."

Smiling and nodding, Fiel took Chlammy's hand and wove a rite again. Meanwhile...

"In any case, I doubt that the reason Mr. Sora entrusted us with the downfall of Elven Gard was such a grand and noble one... Why, don't you agree?"

The two then recalled the man's face—his sloppy, slovenly face—and they quoted him together.

""Man...politics, rights...overthrowing a big country is such a pain in the ass. I'll leave it to you guys.""

Smirking, the pair leaped back into the sky.

■■■

An inn on the outskirts of the city. The companions had secured a little room with two parallel beds. Fiel, having removed her hood and changed into her bedclothes, repeated her admonishment.

"Now, Chlammy, tonight you *must* sleep."

"...W-well then, may I...ask one thing?"

"Yes? Why, ask anything you liike."

Chlammy, hugging a pillow, averted her gaze uncomfortably.

"E-err... C-c-could you...sleep with me?" As Fiel's face lit up knowingly, Chlammy blushed and shouted, "N-no! It's just, Sora's memories are keeping me up! S-so I'm thinking of how Sora holds Shiro's— If you held my hand, it might... It's all Sora's fault, you know?!"

"Yes, yes, it's *all* Mr. Sora's fault. Why, then, you don't need to be ashamed. Just like before, if you have a bad dream, you can jump right under my blanket."

"I said… No, it's not like that! *Ngh*, everything—it's all Sora's fault. Why must I…?" And so on—carping on in a low mumble, she went ahead and climbed into Fiel's bed. To Chlammy, as she lay with her back turned, Fiel smiled and spoke.

"Chlammy, is there anything else you want? Why, I could sing a lullaby."

"I suppose I want you to stop teasing me and let me rest."

"Really? Why, you don't want *stroking* or *fluffing*?"

"………………W-well, if you want to."

"Okay! Why, I want to very much, so I'll go ahead!"

At the sensation of Fiel's hand combing her hair, Chlammy felt the tension leave her body. The familiar feeling—from all those times she'd cried—reminded her of the past.

All those days she'd been kept by the Nirvalens as a slave. Even with Fiel on her side—she'd amassed any number of unpleasant memories, and they made her want to cry. Made her want to die. But she'd decided never to feel sorry for herself. She'd held back the tears with all her might, releasing them all in that bed, back in those days, long ago. By now, having touched Sora's memories, the time had long since passed when she should—

"……Chlammy, are you asleep?"

Fiel's voice was soft so as not to wake her friend if she was. It put the stopper on Sora's memories just as they were about to come rushing back.

"…Not yet. What?"

"Mmm, if you can't sleep, I was thinking of talking a bit until you can. Do you mind?"

"…Well, no…but what?"

At the serious tone underscoring Fiel's words, Chlammy nodded, confused.

"Chlammy, why, it seems as if you trust Mr. Sora *unconditionally*."
Fiel whispered with concern. "To be honest, that worries me…"

"…"

"Are the memories Mr. Sora gave you actually real?"

—Sora and Shiro had a Flügel. With the Covenants, it was possible to falsify memories. Perhaps they had forged memories and
given them to Chlammy to manipulate her. That was what Fiel was
implying. But…

"It's possible I'm being tricked, you mean. That does indeed sound
like something Sora would do—"

Chlammy smirked.

"—*would sound like it, rather.*"

Chlammy tittered at Fiel's dubious expression.

"You needn't worry. The one who's overestimating Sora—*is not
me, but you, Fi.*"

—The memory flashed through the back of Chlammy's mind.
Sora's memory was drenched in awful recollections, but now—

"…Hey, Fi, do you know why the word 'genius' exists?"

"…What?"

"It is to maintain that a *puppet* is not a *person*. One who defies
understanding is called a genius. With approval, a genius. Without,
a monster. As spoken by most people, it is actually a slight."

Implying that since it's a different beast from themselves, there's
nothing more to say, the majority comforted themselves thus and
gave up. But that puppet was different.

"Yes, he really was *just a puppet*."

—He was just a dumbass.

"But *he refused to be just a puppet*."

—He admired the real thing he saw before him.

"And then—he endured, suffering in ways from which it would be
hard to believe one could recover."

Chlammy, in her sleepy daze, swam through Sora's memories. A
way to fly without being able to fly—how could you tell whether or
not it was possible? *By trying to fly—and seeing if you fell*: That was the
only way. After falling so many times, his body, his heart shattered—

"...Even so, he stood up. With that silly grin of his, as if nothing had happened."

His heart bleeding, his teeth grinding, looking at his sister, he stood up. In that, the typical image of a genius's *effortlessness*...was nowhere to be found.

—It really is tough to have a smart little sister, isn't it? "Big brother."

"Sora—*is terribly awkward*. And that is why he could catch up—no, even overtake. He stands at a place anyone can reach if they are a person, while being a fool just as he says. As a fool, he has run to catch up with the *real thing* he admired, *enduring*, over and over—just...a fool."

...As Chlammy spoke, Fiel's hand kept stroking her. Guiding her deeper and deeper beneath a state of consciousness.

"What you need is just a little—but to go all the way—you need enough resolve to make one feel faint, and..."

In her submerged consciousness, Chlammy remembered the tournament for the monarchy, Sora's words:

—*When it comes to conflict and slaughter, we're seasoned experts compared to you*—

Visceral memory overlapped the recollection.

—The memory of blood, on a hand,
at which he looked down with vacant eyes—
the memory of a puppet that wanted only to be a person—

"...He really is...just so awkward...*can't even...tell a single lie...* you know..."

"Chlammy?"

...Only the breath of sleep answered. Deep in thought, Fiel stroked the girl, who had drifted off with words still falling from her lips. *One more thing*, she'd murmured, but left the thought incomplete. Fiel pondered, looking at the ceiling. She recalled the man Chlammy had assessed as awkward, incapable of telling a single lie.

—The face of the man who seemed to walk in clothes woven of lies. Bold, frivolous, eliciting caution from all who saw him—

"——Oh…"

Finally, Fiel got there.

"I see… A 'liar who can't lie'… That's what she meant…"

A man whose life even Chlammy deemed awe-inspiring—one who had weathered such experiences.

Why…*would he elicit caution*?

Fiel felt a long-held unease dissipate. Having reached her answer, imagining a future in which Chlammy believed, of which Sora and his sister dreamed, a minute smile spilled across her face. And the ghosts of sleep that had eluded her returned to close her eyes.

I can't wait, she thought. For the first time in a long time—a really and truly long time, too many years to count—she faded into a deep sleep.

⏻ CHAPTER 1
TRIAL

"Fahhhhhhhhhhhhhhhhhhhhhhhhhhh!!"

—The Kingdom of Elkia: the capital, Elkia. The last bastion of Immanity, the lowest ranking of the Ixseeds. Elkia was a country that, until a few months ago, had been on the brink of destruction, backed into the confines of its sole remaining city. Now it had expanded its territory with unprecedented speed, swallowing up the great maritime nation of the Eastern Union. In the castle of this nation, where reformation from kingdom to commonwealth proceeded at a feverish pitch, a shriek rang out.

—For an instant, the harried castle staff froze as if time itself had stopped. But even that was fleeting as the machine quickly ratcheted back into operation as if nothing had happened. Yes—it was business as usual. Everyone was familiar with it by now. *She* must have been screaming again—and most likely with *exceedingly valid cause.* As an unspoken sense of sympathy swept the castle, everyone went back to work.

"Fahhhhhhhh!! This is idiocy! Is this not idiocy? This is idiocy, is it not?!"

The redhead once again put her masterful phraseology on display.

—Stephanie Dola, aka Steph. Head of the house of Dola, ranked a duchess, and granddaughter of the previous king. A princess in the truest sense of the word. This young lady, once so full of grace, now—unequivocally—devoid of it. Perched in a chair, she tore at her hair, looked toward the sky, and wailed.

"...Who's dumb, please?"

Cross-legged on the floor beside Steph, reading a book, sat the Werebeast—Izuna Hatsuse. Estimated age: one digit. A young girl clothed in traditional Japanese style with large ears, like those of a fennec fox, and a tail. The book in her hands was upside down, but Steph had no time to point that out.

"Sora is, Shiro is—no, *I* am!! 'Why, yes, Sir. You needn't worry.'— what was that?! It was imbecilic! *I* am imbecilic!!" Flinging her arms wide, she ranted. "'Go to your grandfather's library and find the true reason the Siren queen sleeps'!! Why, yes, Sir!! Who but an imbecile would say this?! Just how many books did I think there were?! To begin with...!"

She surveyed the shelves filling the walls. Her diatribe skipped a beat.

"Find *a book that may or may not even exist*? Just what did I think I was agreeing to?!"

The two young women were in the hidden room left by the previous king—his secret study. The former ruler had always played the fool to reveal the truth behind the games of other countries—other races with magic and supernatural powers—and the strategies that would allow a mere human to overcome them. The records on which he had staked his life—the legacy of a great man—were arrayed along those walls. His feats were chronicled in tomes easily exceeding a thousand volumes, which filled the study. Though the books were arranged in chronological order, without any clue as to when the old king had interacted with the Sirens, the girls' only choice was to power through all the books by brute force. Belated recognition of this fact had prompted Steph's scream—mere moments earlier. But more than that— Almost crying, she thrust a finger at Izuna, the little Werebeast girl holding her book upended.

"Just how did Sora think you could help? You *can't even read* Immanity!"

"Stuch...pipe down, please. The hell you think I'm working on right now, please?"

—*Excuse me?*

"W-wait, can we back up? What did you just call me?"

"...? Goddamn Gramps said, 'Steph is a duchess,' please?"

"Why do you have to abbreviate it further?! It sounds horribly belittling!"

"...How the hell's that, please, Stuch?" Izuna cocked her head and peered up at Steph.

"A-aaaaaaahh, could you please not insult me with such round eyes?! How will you make it up to me if my sleep deprivation curses me by opening up another secret door?!"

Steph writhed, banging her head on the corner of a desk, but Izuna replied calmly.

"Stuch, shut it and work, please. Gramps is waiting, please."

"...Mg-ghh...... Y-yes, I suppose so. Grieving will accomplish nothing."

Indeed. Siren had taken a hostage, Izuna's grandfather Ino Hatsuse. Izuna must have been tired, too. There was no time for Steph to waste wailing while Izuna struggled to learn an unfamiliar writing system. *Yes, take a deep breath.* Regaining her composure, Steph finally broke the news.

"By the way, Miss Izuna...your book is upside down."

"......! I-I know that, please. Y-you think I'd do that by mistake, please?!"

Izuna scrambled to right her book as Steph set about lecturing her.

"And, perhaps you've got this already, but Immanity's tongue, unlike Werebeast's, is written horizontally."

"—? There are languages written horizontally, please?" Izuna's "The hell?" face consisted of a wide-eyed gape.

"...Miss Izuna, come to think of it, I have yet to hear: How old are you?"

At this, Izuna started counting on her fingers before uneasily asking:

"Do...do I count from zero, please?"

—Steph grasped it. Indeed, it was no wonder that Izuna was fond of Sora and Shiro. They were of entirely the *same breed*. Genius gamers, oblivious to all else. With a sigh, Steph pointed to another book.

"Miss Izuna, I suggest you begin there."

"The hell's this, please?"

"That is the textbook I used in school to learn the Werebeast tongue. It is a bilingual game—"

"—Mmph. Understood, please."

As soon as she heard the word *game*, Izuna seized the book and started flipping through the pages. Steph had to credit her effort. It was clear she was doing her best. But what could she read at that speed—? Steph sighed at the ceiling.

"I...in any case, I suppose there is no option but to go through all the books—"

Just as Steph arrived at this tragic conclusion—*grmmmmmmmgl-grgl*—a sound (and the words that followed) sent her resolution up in smoke.

"—Stuch, I'm goddamn hungry, please. Feed me, please."

As if a switch had been flipped, Izuna thumped her book closed. She had plenty of drive and motivation—and of course she would make the effort to save her grandfather. But, *leaving that aside*, Izuna's voluminous eyes demanded, without a hint of malice: *Feed me.* The young girl scratched her large animal ears with her foot, her big tail swaying to and fro. The adorable sight pressed Steph to make a decision:

    1.   Forget it all and just faint already.

    2.   Prepare a meal for this unbearably lovable beast.

At the end of her reflection, her need for sleep bowed to the power of cute.

"A-all right… When you're hungry, you're hungry… I'll whip something up with what I've got on hand."

"Mm, I want fish, but I'll suck it up and let you off the hook, please."

And so Steph slumped off as if dragging her feet behind her.

…By the way, do you remember that they were still in Elkia Castle? Steph was spectacularly forgetting that she had the option of just fainting already and leaving it to the cooks to prepare a meal for Izuna. But as Steph shambled on like a ghost with Izuna in tow, wagging her big tail, no one was there to remind them.

■■■

Meanwhile—*twenty thousand meters above sea level.* Beset by winds one encounters at an altitude triple that of the Himalayas, Sora wondered how to describe the sight stretching out before him.

—First, try imagining a Rubik's Cube. Take that intellectual puzzle and hand it to someone of severely limited intellect. Soon—dismantled with pliers, countless pieces of what once had been a Rubik's Cube would be scattered across the floor. Now, please suppress the urge to comment, and repeat this process about a thousand times more. How about it? Can you imagine it? The landscape that would emerge from this exercise—was basically what Sora saw.

"Welcome to my homeland, constructed on the back of a Phantasma. The city of the heavens—Avant Heim!"

There towered the mountain of dismembered Rubik's Cubes. Sora rolled his eyes and muttered as Jibril, smiling happily, pronounced this a "city."

"Hey, the cities we know, if I remember correctly, at least have roads."

A vista woven of countless giant cubes stacked haphazardly one atop another. Viewed by an avant-garde artist, perhaps some sublime theme would emerge. Unfortunately, Sora—a virginal eighteen-year-old layman—if asked to describe it could only come up with one word. Namely—*chaos.*

"Okay, Jibril—for now, we have just one thing to suggest to the Flügel."

"...Structures should be...accessible..."

—Parting ways with Steph and Izuna, Sora and the rest had set off to ascertain the true conditions to wake the Siren queen. To study records of past games, they turned to the world's greatest storehouse of knowledge—the city of Flügel, Avant Heim.

"Oh, Master. Please stay close to me. The air is a bit thin here."

Sora and Shiro nodded at Jibril's warning. Sora had no idea how they could have moved anyway.

"...Well, I guess if it's just Flügel living here, they don't need any infrastructure..."

The city splayed below them had no roads, doors, or windows. It made sense that a species that could move practically without limit would have no need of such things, but an urban landscape comprised of endless cubes defied perspective. Without a point of reference, everything lacked scale.

"...Not like a city...more like a puzzle..."

Shiro, having made this blunt assessment, looked up and whispered:

"...The sky is...blue?"

At twenty thousand meters, they should have already been at space's doorstep. The sky shouldn't have been blue...

"Avant Heim is a member of Ixseed Rank Two, Phantasma. Higher than Rank Three, Elemental, the spirits that feed the corridors from which this world is woven. It is a living being independent of ordinary ecosystems. Put simply...you may think of Avant Heim as a *discrete world*."

Though it seems the atmospheric pressure is insufficient for you, my masters, Jibril went on to explain.

""Hmm...I see—not.""

Sora and Shiro nodded together, their expressions blank.

"It's kinda refreshing, in a way, how resolute both Flügel and Phantasma are about defying comprehension."

Sora tossed off a sarcastic jab. Shifting his line of sight to the distance, at the foot of an unusually tall tree—it was…it was, wasn't it? Something that looked for all the world like a dragon skull, enshrined in neat, ribboned decoration—

"…Jibril. I do not get the design concept of this city at all."

"What?! How distressing, that the land destined to enthrone my masters should fail to suit their tastes…"

Sora cradled his head and groaned at this response from Jibril, who looked slightly dejected.

"By the way, you think it's about time we save this twerp?" Sora pointed to—

"Eeyauuuuugh, the sun, the suuun! I'm meltiiing! I'm smoking and frying and meltiiinnggg!"

—Plum, who had her cape pulled up over her and was curled into a small, wildly shrieking ball.

"Oh, how regrettable…I forgot about you entirely. Are you still alive?"

"I'll be dead in a few secooonds! I feel my power drainiiing!"

Plum was a Dhampir, to whom sunlight was lethal. Apparently, she'd somehow been able to manage using magic, but it seemed magic was now being consumed at an unexpectedly high clip.

"So yeah, Jibril. We don't wanna keep Izuna waiting forever, so take us quick to wherever's got the most info. And, considering Plum, it would be ideal if it was indoors—"

"Your wish is my command. Please place your hands on me once more. And also…"

With a somehow meek, complicated expression, she clasped Sora's and Shiro's hands.

"…Masters. I am well aware it is not my place to do so—but may I ask of you *just two things*?"

"…What's all this? You don't gotta be all humble like that…"

"—Please *do not despair of me*. And please *have faith in me*." …That was pretty cryptic. But Jibril left it at that and continued, "You, there."

"Y-yeeeess?!"

In response, Plum, now known as "You There," peeped out from under her cape with bloodshot eyes.

"I would not mind leaving you behind...but would you please hurry and take hold of me?"

"Uhhh, yes, I'm coming. Don't leave without—" Plum scrambled up, and the instant she touched Jibril—the scenery changed.

███

It was probably the interior of one of the cubes they'd seen from afar. A library—even greater and more majestic than the Elkia Grand National Library, which Jibril had privatized. The ceiling was high, and the structure suggested a well hole formed by excavating the inside of a ten-story building. The interior was like the ruins of an ancient city: stairs and columns of stone stacked without cracks, intricate passageways and arched bridges with vines clinging to their surfaces.

But—what appeared to be pillars of stone were, in fact, bookcases.

Various unidentifiable knickknacks also littered the landscape. Stairs and suspension bridges traced unthinkable patterns, like illusory Escher illustrations—all lit by giant skylights that were surely invisible from the outside, as well as countless lanterns that floated without support.

It was fantastic and beautiful, even as it defied human understanding—a library of blasphemy (or something). But for now, there was something else on Sora's mind, which he indicated with a jab of his finger.

"...Jibril, I'm guessing this is your doing?"

It was probably because Jibril had warped them in along with the air they needed. The library (or whatever) raged with gales that sent reams of books spiraling through the cavernous structure. Nevertheless, Jibril watched the havoc she'd wreaked with a prim smile.

"Trouble yourself not, Master. The owner of this place is the one who approved the Book Sharing Act."

Sora recalled why Jibril had snatched up the Elkia Grand National

Library—no, fled Avant Heim—as he watched the books convulsing. The books in Avant Heim had accumulated close to overflowing, and to address this, the Book Sharing Act had been passed in the name of *eliminating redundancy.*

"Her books are the Flügel's books. I am a Flügel. Therefore her books are my books."

With a syllogism tight enough to justify the bullying in *Dora*mon,* she grinned.

"One aware that I might make such a careless slip—perhaps even intentionally?—while passing such a generous law must clearly be endowed with a heart so magnanimous as to overlook this trifle. Even if these pages include grimoires and prohibited books that cannot be copied or duplicated—or originals without the like anywhere in the world. Yes, I'm sure. ♥"

Oh. So if they were her books, she could wreck them.

—The real issue seemed to be that Jibril really couldn't get past that Book Sharing Act she'd rebelled against before. Then—

"Nyaaaahhhh! My books! Books I haven't finished readiiing!!"

Eyes gathered in the direction of this wail. And there—

"…Wow…"

—they found a girl even Shiro softly exclaimed at, a girl of literally inhuman beauty. The halo revolving above her head and the wings protruding from her hips made it clear that she was a Flügel, just like Jibril. But her halo spun in a pattern quite a bit more complex than Jibril's. Most notably, from her jade hair protruded a single horn. Her form, as she flitted through the air on the motion of wings seemingly made of light, was incomparably divine. But her visage as she flew about, scooping up her books while seemingly on the verge of tears, lacked the inorganic quality they'd perceived in Jibril on their first meeting—one might even have called this girl cute.

—*Hff, hff.* Panting with an air of affectation, she flitted over to Jibril. "Ngghh, Jibs, you're such a meanie!"

She screwed up her face sullenly, but her expression quickly rebounded with an angelic smile.

"Or, wait! Is it as they say—when you like someone, you tease them? Ngmm, Jibs! Welcome baaaack, tee-hee!"

Leaping for an embrace, the girl found herself spectacularly side-stepped as Jibril shifted out of the way. Standing behind Sora and Shiro and watching her admirer smash into a mountain of books, Jibril spoke neutrally.

"...Master, let me introduce you. This Flügel is the chair of the Avant Heim government, the very one who approved the most loathsome law under the sky, the Book Sharing Act. She is the Alipotentiary, the final decision-maker—"

And Jibril heaved a sigh.

"—my elder, Azril."

Such was the introduction of the motionless girl with her torso buried in a pile of books.

...

"......How do I put this...?"

"...You Flügel...are interesting..."

This was Rank Six. A race that was once a weapon used to kill gods, sowing death wheresoever they went—and this was their acting agent plenipotentiary? Sora and Shiro mumbled rather forced reactions to this revelation.

Perhaps likewise shifting, the girl, who had been partially entombed in books, made a transition invisible to Sora & Co., and was now hanging on their companion, rubbing her cheek against Jibril's.

"Eee, Jibs, you're so *naughty*! Here I was so excited you finally showed up again, and then you treat me like thiiiiis— **Oh, but! That's your charm!!**"

"And I see you have not changed, Elder Azril. You are as disgusting as ever."

While her cheek was being polished, Jibril delivered her comment through unbent lips.

—Not one of her usual sardonic jibes, but a direct insult. However.

"Nyah, I'm not your elder, I'm your *big sister.* How many times do I have to tell you, nya-haaa?!"

Azril flew through the air in a figure eight, quickly resuming her glomping of Jibril.

"Jibril was one thing, but those Flügel, are they really cool with having this chick as their agent plenipotentiary?"

"...Are you...one to talk...?" Shiro quipped sarcastically, but no one paid heed.

Meanwhile, the jowl-abused Jibril pointedly pushed on. "Elder Azril, I have come today with a request, that you allow my masters to peruse this—"

"I refuse. I refuse until you call me big sister!"

As if aggravated from the heart, Jibril conceded.

"...If you explain why you continue to caress my cheek and permit my masters to view your materials, I shall consider it."

"'Cos you're so cute, Jibs! Explanation done, permission given!! Now say it: big sister! ♥"

As Azril's arms came in for her embrace, Jibril shifted deftly away.

"Now, Masters, we have permission, so please make yourself at home. This is the collection of the Alipotentiary. It includes countless books appropriated through abuse of that loathsome law. I surmise that there be no greater assemblage of knowledge."

"H-how could you?! Jibs, you broke the promise you made with your big sister?!"

As Azril's jaw dropped in exaggerated despair, Jibril answered with the finest of smiles, "I said I would consider it. *I considered it* and decided against it!"

"Nggh, I didn't think you were such a tricky little kid, Jibs. Who's been giving you ideas, I wonder?"

—*Staaaaaare.* Daggers launched through tears pierced Sora & Co. Under the pressure of a gaze seemingly capable of crushing the life from a body—

"Yo, I'm Sora. This is my sister, Shiro. Nice to meet ya."

"...Hey..."

—the siblings responded disinterestedly, already used to this sort of thing with Jibril.

Pointing to Azril as she let out a curious *Hmm?*, Sora moved on. "But anyway. 'Big sister'? You mean Jibril is the little sister of the Flügel's agent plenipotentiary?"

"Bingo! ♥"

"Quite the contrary! ♪"

Instantly—and bearing the expressions of real sisters—the two responded both simultaneously and in diametric opposition. With a sigh, Jibril expounded coolly:

"Flügel do not procreate. We have neither sisters nor parents. It is simply a matter of precedence of birth."

"...Oh, so that's what you mean by 'elder.'"

In other words, she'd been created before Jibril.

"Elder Azril, by the way, is the Alipotentiary and not the agent plenipotentiary."

"...What's the difference?"

"She is merely the chair of the Council of Eighteen Wings, consisting of nine Flügel, including her."

Now that she mentioned it, Sora remembered. Jibril had been a member of that Council before becoming his and Shiro's property, hadn't she?

"She has, for what it's worth, the right to make the final decision in such extraordinary circumstances as call for it, as well as certain other privileges, but—"

To sum up—*hff.* Jibril shook her head and smirked.

"*She is neither superior nor great*, and thus, there is no particular need to revere her."

"...You're even harsh to your own guys. You've really got that shtick down..."

But as if dissatisfied with that assessment, Azril puffed out her cheeks and rebutted. "Nooo!! We were all created by Lord Artosh, so our father is Lord Artosh, and I'm your big sister 'cos I was created first! You were created last, Jibs, so you're my little sister! Isn't it obvious?!"

Going past smirk territory all the way into a sneer, Jibril objected, "—Raising said argument in the Council, this individual of unfortunate intellect found her proposal rejected unanimously."

"Buuut! There was no other way I could get you to call me big sister!"

"And the Council rejected your proposal in appalled recognition of this motive. Surely you must have heard?"

As Jibril continued in an even colder tone, Azril glommed on to her once more and commenced her smiling sister-bragging.

"You know, there was a bunch of kids who were made toward the end of the War, but Jibs is the ultimate, the Closing Number."

Nya-ha-ha-ha, she chortled, while Jibril sighed as if feeling deeply inconvenienced.

"And those kids made at the end…*believe* me, that was when Lord Artosh was at the height of his power, so to even compare them with those of us made earlier—that's a laugh!! But then, guess what? All those strong kids got tossed out on the front lines—and they *all died* in the Final Battle…"

The crestfallen Azril accosted her sole surviving sister, hugging her with a force that would probably burst an Immanity like a balloon.

"So Jibs is the one and only late-period Flügel who survived the Final Battle, and on top of that, she's the Closing Number! The youngest of us all, the cutie-pie little sister! This ought to be spelled out by law! Why don't they *understand*?"

Azril once more took flight in a merry figure eight. Jibril was also something of a sight, squinting in an uncharacteristic display of displeasure, but—

"…That at-a-loss…expression…on Jibril… This is rare footage…"

Shiro recorded the angels' antics with her phone. Meanwhile, Sora was pursuing an alternate train of thought.

Intently observing Azril's *innocent, glowing smile*: "…Aw, damn. Guess we might have to change our plans…," he *muttered with affected disappointment*.

—*Glare*. Azril turned at these soft words with a smile—but eyes laden with violent force.

"—So is it *you* who's been screwing around with our lovely Jibs?"

"Heh, *you ask a virgin about screwing around*? That's a tough question you've thrown out there."

Sora thrust out his chest with tragic conviction. Azril took a step forward.

"Whoa—..."

"...Ng?"

There was no way to react. Her step ignored distance. Sora and Shiro, who took several moments to even realize they'd been approached, groaned softly.

—Just then, a silent impact spread from Jibril to rock the entire library. Suspecting the use of magic, Sora came to a sudden realization, listening to the following exchange between the two Flügel.

"...My *elder*, if you plan to lay a finger on my masters—I ask that you reconsider carefully."

"Oh, come on, Jibs, *you don't have to warn me like that*. We've got the Ten Covenants, you know?"

It had been a *subtle display of hostility*. At this hint of just how much Jibril was curbing her power under usual circumstances—this mere hint of Jibril's true potential—a cold sweat ran down Sora's and Shiro's cheeks. Brushing off this "subtle" display, Azril turned back to Sora. Jade eyes—strangely, entirely different in nature from Jibril's—pierced him.

"There's just one thing I want to clarify."

"—Mm, what is it?"

—There was no comparing this glare to the one she'd leveled at him earlier. Its weight was sufficient to coagulate the air of the library, to make space itself creak. Say the wrong thing—and you were dead.

This world had the Ten Covenants. Jibril was attendant beside him. Yet none of that helped. That was the illusion her eyes evoked. Azril spoke.

"...Will Jibs call me 'big sister ♥' if you command it?"

...

………?

An anticlimax—no, a letdown so massive it gave the sense that your soul might fly off if you didn't cling to it. Sora only managed to keep his feet thanks to the sensation of Shiro's trembling hand grasping his. But Azril seemed oblivious as she went on upping the voltage.

"A-and you even got her to lick the feet of an E-E-Elf! Could you get her to lick m-my… O-or take a bath with me? N-no, I'm not asking thaaat much! If you could just show me—"

—How did she know that much? Sora wondered, but for now, he slipped out his phone and told her to see for herself.

"…Jibril's bath scene? I do have a clip or—"

"I bet the Flügel Piece! Give it to meee!"

—Twenty thousand meters in the air, an unlikely thunder roared.

"*Miss* Azril, please cool your head. *Madam*, you have no such authority. Should you wish to wager the Race Piece, would not the first step be to bring it to a vote in the Council? Though such a proposal would surely be unanimously rejected. ♥"

Jibril gave a scornful smile such as Sora and Shiro had never seen before.

"Ngh, nghhhh…! —Nyah?"

At the notes of Jibril's voice containing a silent "lol," Azril exclaimed:

"Wait… My brains are revving up hard enough to roar! They're being activated to levels never before seen in the twenty-six-thousand-year history of Azril! They're spinning at the speed of light!"

—Dropping her unbelievable age, Azril apparently dove into thought. Finally with what came across as a flash of insight, she raised her head frantically.

"—That's it! You're…Sora, right?!"

"Uh, yeah."

"I'll be your property, too! Then I bet I can get in the bath with Jibs!!"

"Congratulations on spinning at speed unprecedented in twenty-six thousand years without driving anywhere, *Miss* Azril."

Jibril sneered with a smirk colder than cold, even a hint of disappointment. *But*—Shiro glanced quietly at her brother. Azril had offered herself up just like that—but, as Jibril had said, she wasn't the agent plenipotentiary. Getting her wouldn't get them Flügel. But to play Flügel in a game would be no simple matter. It wouldn't be a bad move to grab Azril while she was hinting she might lose on purpose. Especially considering that part of Sora's objective was to swallow up Flügel. With these thoughts, Shiro looked to her brother's face for confirmation—

"...?"

But, at Sora's expression, disinterested and aloof, she tilted her head and considered Azril again. That smile, as enchanting as ever—just *too* perfect—

"...Ahh..." Shiro subtly nodded in recognition of what Sora's bearing conveyed. And of course, Sora then shrugged and turned away.

"...Sorry to bow out now, but let's come back to this later..."

"Whaaaaaat...? I wanted to see Jibs *naked*—"

Ignoring Azril as she champed at them, Sora took Shiro's hand and heaved a deep sigh.

"...Man, I was all up on Steph about how we were going to get three races, but I guess I'm gonna have to tell her sorry." He cast a look at Azril with eyes disappointed to their depths. "*This bitch is useless*. Jibril's enough."

Ignoring Azril's gaze, which was narrowing in their direction, Sora and Shiro headed for the mountainous stacks.

"So, Jibril. We can look at all these books, right?"

"...Yes. After all, we did just receive permission from Elder Azril herself."

Nodding, Sora looked around. Books, books, books... It was like a giant town made of nothing but books. In his current field of vision—multiple languages he couldn't read graced the spines.

"*Since we didn't get what we wanted*, looks like the going's gonna be tough... Well, we'll do what we can, huh, Shiro?"

"...Mm."

As the siblings disappeared into the stacks, the two Flügel watched them in silence.

■■■

Sitting cross-legged atop one of the mountains of books, chin in hand:

"Mmm, I thought I could get you back by using myself as bait, Jibs. But I guess my hook was too big?"

With a chilly smile, Azril mumbled the reason *Sora didn't get what he wanted*. Indeed, contrary to the attitude she presented, she didn't trust or respect Sora and Shiro in the slightest. She'd only been thinking of how to trap them in order to get Jibril back.

—*Without showing any interest in why Jibril deferred to them as her masters.*

"...You never change, do you, *Azril*?"

Azril flinched at being addressed merely by name, but her reply was composed.

"It doesn't make any sense that you, who were always so cheeky to me and even Lord Artosh, would grovel before mere Immanities. Just use the Covenants, and it should be easy to negate their wills, or even turn them into puppets. I mean, I know you must have lost to them by some fluke and been forced to serve them. I can see—"

She peered deep into Jibril's eyes—

"—you've changed, Jibs."

At Azril's words, Jibril smiled coldly.

"Indeed. I have been able to change...*unlike you, who never can*."

"......"

"You fail to consider even the possibility that I *was challenged and then lost*—I suppose I should not have expected more." Icily, and with a distant, betrayed smile, Jibril went on. "...I turned my cheek to you and our departed lord alike because I could not bear to watch. You are too hardheaded. And that is why..."

A moment's hesitation. Should she say it, or—? But Jibril made up her mind and opened her mouth, knowing that Azril was more painfully aware of this than anyone. But even so, judging that it needed saying, she unleashed the words.

"That is why we failed, and that is why—you still cannot change."

This simple assertion was enough to strip away Azril's affected smile. With the face of a puppet devoid of truth, of warmth, Azril—no, *something that looked like Azril*—queried:

"—Jibril, mean'st thou to say thou hast found the Answer?"

Repulsed by *that thing* in front of her, Jibril spat her reply.

"—Yes. To be precise, I found it a long time ago. I only lacked proof."

"......"

"Now, I need to assist my masters in their search—so if you'll excuse me."

Leaving *it* to its silence, Jibril turned on her heel.

——......

"What do you think?"

—That is a question.

"...Hmmm, what if she's wrong?"

—That is no question.

"...Well, yeah..."

—Azril, first of our number, I leave the decision to you. Not only myself, but *we all have*.

"...I know, okay?"

She knew. She reminded herself of it once more. Azril responded to the will of Avant Heim within her. She watched the figures rummaging through the books—though she would have to bide her time for them to attack again—and then, she would and ask.

■■■

"...Damn it, we don't have time for this."

After a mere thirty minutes or so in the shadow of those looming mountains of books, Sora realized this was a futile endeavor.

"Shiro, how many of this world's languages have you learned?"

"...Immanity, Elf, Werebeast...that's all."

Shiro mumbled apologetically, but Sora rubbed her head tenderly. To Sora, for whom Immanity was as far as he could go, "That's all" was something he'd never say. Her ability to absorb information was dizzying. But even so—

"Jibril, what languages are these?"

"Those would be the Dwarven and Demonia tongues. I can read them, but—"

...Yes, Jibril was the only one who could read all these books. Shiro might have been able to pick up new languages with improbable speed, but one couldn't even imagine how many millions of books confronted them. It was impossible to dig up the information they needed with a workforce of this scale, *and they'd known that perfectly well from the beginning.*

"...Jibril."

"Yes?"

"There's no time. If we keep mucking around here, Ino's gonna be in danger. We may have bought ourselves some insurance, but if those broads start thinking we really ran away, that's no good— Can you round up some labor?"

They couldn't be sitting around here forever, gathering information. Sooner or later, they'd have to take on the queen again. So their original plan had been to use Azril to gather stuff—but when they discovered that she *had absolutely no such intention,* they knew they weren't getting what they wanted. Sora had seen Azril's face. It didn't represent the Flügel Sora had imagined based on what he knew—utterly devoid of Jibril's intellectual curiosity and fighting spirit. It was—just—

"...I can, but I surmise it will turn out *just as you guess.*"

Yeah, exactly what Azril wanted—but.

"Screw it, we gotta. We don't have time to hem and haw—Shiro."

"...Mm."

Biting his nails—an unusual habit for him, even when nervous— Sora put aside his muttering and, with Shiro's attention, plowed forward.

"—Now that we've missed our mark, we're gonna have to improvise. I'm counting on you to pick it up."

"...Okay..."

■■■

"Hey, Az...ril?"

Sora had steeled his determination before speaking but stammered for a moment nonetheless.

—She must have materialized some scenery from the Eastern Union, stuff she'd read about. Like the Japanese shut-ins Sora knew (in other words, Shiro and him), she sat deep in a heated *kotatsu* table, wearing a blanket over her head, watching a screen displaying only static—

"...What do you want...? You need a *useless* kid like me?"

What a waste of effort... Azril had cloaked her immediate surroundings in darkness and was putting it all into an emotional appeal. Finding the stench of her acting impressive in its own way, Sora's expression was strained.

"Uhh...um...you know how the Sirens have this queen who's, like, passed out?"

Azril answered, still bundled in her blanket. "Nya-ha... That dumb kid who got inspired by some stupid fairy tale to drive two entire races, including her own, to the brink of extinction in a single generation. She's so stupid, even the shellfish clam up. Everyone knows her..."

...Unable to describe the impression of watching Azril's halo spinning above her blanket, Sora continued, "Y-yeah, that chick. We're looking for records of the covenant she set forth for her game."

"...Even Jibs knows that. 'I'm gonna sleep until you make me fall in love' or something."

"Yeah, but—that was actually bullshit."

At Sora's words, seemingly forgetting her tear-jerking efforts, Azril's eyes lit up.

"Huhh! That's why everyone failed? So what was it really?"

—Despite everything, she was a Flügel after all.

"That's what we want to find out. So we want to gather records of the queen's game as it's been played in the past, the stuff the players were told, as much as possible. And then we'll compare it all."

"Hmmm..."

After gazing into space for a while, Azril answered curtly:

"Well, if you just need records, they've gotta be here somewhere, so have at it. Let me know when you figure it out."

Flügel maybe, but *very unlike Jibril indeed.*

"Yeah, but there are too many. We don't have time to go through them all. Don't you know where—?"

"No idea! Ah-ha-ha-ha-ha!"

......

"It's the Sharing Act, y'know! After all those rounds of borrowing and lending, I can't even guess where they are by now."

"Do you see now, Master? This is why I fled my homeland."

Discarding her emotional appeal, Azril beamed while Jibril glowered.

"...You guys, if your life is collecting books, at least organize them..."

"Mm? Nah, you've got it wrong. We collect knowledge. Books, who cares? Once I've got one memorized, I could even just toss it for all I care, but then the kids who haven't read it would get all pissed."

Smiling as though on the verge of committing an assault, Jibril spelled it out once more. "Do you see now, Master? *This* is why I fled my homeland."

—*Hmm,* Sora thought, getting the picture. All that really mattered was knowledge—and *that meant...* It was a total joke, but he glossed over it. "So what should we do?"

"Well, I guess you should go find the kids who know where the books are? There are some serious ones like Jibs. If you're motivated, you can probably dig 'em all up, y'know."

"Hmm, then get us—"

"I don't feel like it."

Slipping back into her calculated self-pity, Azril pulled the blanket back over her head.

"If it's just Jibs's favorite toys mucking around, I can look the other way, but who says I have to help you? I don't gain anything by making friends with you, and Jibs is calling me stupid, even. I'm *so* depressed right now. I'm so *hurt*, I don't feel like doing anything."

Sora slowly withdrew his phone. "Even if I tell you I'll show you footage of Jibril in the bath?"

"———Forget it."

"If you act now, I'll throw in the right to be called 'big sister.'"

"———————————————F-forget…it."

Azril broke into a sweat as if just emerging from some sort of fierce battle. Heaving her shoulders as if being tried unforgivingly, she squeezed out a voice.

"L-look, I'm *reaaaaally* hurt right now— A-and you think something like that— Wait, I don't mean to call the video of Jibs 'something like that.' I just mean my wounds are even deeper than—I mean, you know…you know what I mean, right?"

Tsk— Sora silently clucked. He'd figured that, among all the lies and performance, at least *her obsession with Jibril was real*, but his trump card failed to do the trick. Now his opponent was in total control. Play Flügel? At an unknown game, while they had the upper hand—? You jest.

"—Honestly, all it means to me if the lot of you small fries, mangy mutts, and hairless monkeys go to ruin is that there will be a few new books about it. In fact, that's really better as far as I'm concerned."

She glared at Sora intently.

"For those of us who live forever…you chumps who die in the blink of an eye aren't good for much more than another silly fairy tale. Help you? What makes you think I should go to the trouble?"

—But he wouldn't let Azril and Flügel take the lead. If they did, Sora and Shiro were finished. If Azril was in it for the mind games—then great.

"Yeah, I guess that's how it is. That's why I said you're *useless*, but I guess you don't get sarcasm, do you, you walking corpse?"

At Sora's brazen comeback—Azril's expression moved.

"*A tool with no one to use you. A puppet without a master.* What a fun eternity that must be."

"—..."

"Whatever. Asshats like you just wait for us to take over the world and then come whining, 'Let us join you,' right? All you know how to do is jump on the bandwagon. We'll handle it with Jibril. Scout out your people one by one—"

Sora turned to leave.

"...You think you can pick a fight with me and then run?" Azril demanded.

We got her, Sora snickered to himself.

"A fight? Ha, it's not a fight if you're not even on the same level."

"Huh...it's nice to see you know."

"—Dude, you're obviously the one outclassed. Get your head out of your ass, you birdbrain."

"...Excellent. Let's do this."

Raising her hands, Azril bellowed down at Sora and Shiro.

"Wish, and it shall be thine—if thou but kill its owner!"

...

—...Shiro's and Sora's eyes narrowed at this epic BS.

"...What's that from...?"

"Oh, Master, this is a Flügel proverb. It is quite understandable that you would not know it."

"Hey, that's not even the issue here!"

"We're not gonna fight—we're gonna play. But—"

Ignoring Sora and Jibril's exchange, Azril snapped her fingers.

"If you want the help of everyone Jibs knows, you'll have to take them all on."

—That instant, everyone present was shifted by a coercive power even Jibril could not defy. And above their new location...

...hung a banner that read: "   " Autograph and Handshake

SESSION. Countless Flügel were busily engaged there, working hard on setup for the event—

"…Damn it—!!"

From the hundred looks that turned his way all at once, Sora instantly grasped everything.

—Her taking his bait was an act—i.e., *she'd outmanipulated him.* But this shock paled in comparison to all the eyes now upon them, which caused Sora and Shiro to black out momentarily. But—a question plaguing Sora allowed him to just barely retain his grip on consciousness. He hadn't seen this card coming at all. Sora couldn't hear as he took his unconscious posture. He'd already shut his ears, but squeals were undoubtedly bursting around him. As countless gazes descended, Sora asked in a trembling voice:

"Hey, Jibril. What is…this? What the hell is *this*?"

Guarding Shiro as her eyes rolled back in her head, Sora screamed, but Jibril merely clapped her hands—

"Oh, I had forgotten entirely. In order to place pressure on the Eastern Union, I have been preaching the good news that I have observed and set down. As it is the most efficient method of evangelism—"

—and beamed.

"I have spread tickets for autographs, tickets for dates, tickets to lie alongside you. All kinds and all manner of fantastic extras—"

"Knock off the dirty business!! That's just gonna get the crazies to buy 'em all and no one else!"

"…I see. I wondered why the turnout was so small, given the number of tickets distributed. But that would explain it, I suppose. Next time, then, I shall devise a more efficient method of promotion—excuse me, evangelism."

While a straight-faced Jibril scribbled notes or something in a book, Sora railed:

"Look, Jibril! If you're going to pull shit like this, at least let me know!!"

—And that would explain how Azril weirdly knew so much about them. But how were you supposed to out bet the opponent on a blind spot *your own guys couldn't see*?! Anyway, it looked as if the nigh–one hundred Flügel crowded about were their fans. As Sora once more went faint at the attention, Jibril continued with a smile—

"Fear not, Master. This hand is yours."

"Wha...uh, what?"

—and with these words, turned her sharp gaze to Azril.

"꒐꒐꒐꒐꒐꒐꒐꒐꒐꒐꒐꒐꒐꒐꒐"

"꒐꒐꒐꒐꒐꒐꒐꒐꒐꒐꒐꒐꒐"

"꒐꒐꒐꒐꒐꒐꒐꒐꒐꒐꒐꒐꒐꒐"

"꒐꒐꒐꒐꒐꒐꒐꒐꒐꒐꒐꒐"

—The Flügel tongue, perhaps? Jibril and Azril exchanged words incomprehensible to Sora and Shiro. But for some reason, the hall—so recently filled with squeals—transformed into a square of tense silence.

"...Excuse me, Miss Jibril? I've got a bad feeling about this, but what did you just say?"

"Oh, my apologies, Master. Now that the matter is settled, I shall explain."

Jibril turned back and continued, "Let us accept Elder Azril's suggestion and have these maids assist us in our search." She smiled at the quivering Sora and Shiro. "All we must do is to defeat them all in a game!"

"Jibril, do you realize how hard it was to beat just you? You think we can take them all?"

"...*Chatter chatter shiver shiver...*"

Sora and Shiro were already petrified of crowds and being objects of attention. If on top of that they had to play *Materialization Shiritori* with practically a hundred Flügel, they were done for. Imagining this—Sora and Shiro went white.

"No, you see, you must merely defeat them all in one swoop. It is a blessedly merciful demand."

"That's right. You're gonna play them all."

"As it has been settled, if you win, they will all collect the books that contain the content you seek. Whereas, if you lose, they will receive autographs, handshakes, and, well, all those things they want."

Squeeeeeeeeeeeeeeeeeeeeeeeeeeeeeee! As squeals rolled over the venue, the blanched Sora and Shiro went limp.

"Jibril...are you asking us to die...?"

"...Jibril...I...believed, in you..."

"Please, be at ease. It is inconceivable, after all, that you would lose, my masters. And by the way..." Jibril consoled the siblings as they shivered like newborn gazelles.

And she turned back to Azril, who clapped her hands...

"This is too many kids to play *shiritori*—let's play tag."

"—Jibril, I'll say it again—are you asking us to die?"

"...*Shiver shiver shiver shiver...*"

—Play tag against Flügel? As if there was anywhere they could escape these psychos, who could fly and warp freely. She must have been telling them indirectly, *Go on ahead to the next world.* But Azril cut their thoughts short.

"But it wouldn't be any fun just playing tag—if we're gonna play..."

"Like true Flügel—we should incorporate wordplay."

Thus declared, Jibril extended her hand. And over it—swirling—appeared forty-six syllables bathed in light. Familiar syllables—forty-six generated from their language. Jibril tossed them to Azril.

"Hmmm? These are from your world? Are these plucked from your native syllables?"

Azril studied them, moving her hand intricately.

—Sora and Shiro couldn't sense it, but judging by the rattle of the ground beneath them, they could tell a gigantic rite had gone *whooom*.

"Mm, all done. Let's get going, okay?"

With that, the syllables vanished from Azril's hand.

—All at once, they scattered, individually settling at random upon any of the nigh–one hundred Flügel girls. Having confirmed this, Azril said:

"The rules are simple. Each syllable has now been transcribed *somewhere* on a different girl's body."

—Forty-six syllables. Nearly a hundred participants. No way to tell who had which.

"The game is tag. I'll be nice and say they can't shift, as a handicap."

—And.

"If you two get caught by these kids, you lose. If you can keep going without getting caught for an hour, you win."

"If you touch one of the transcribed syllables—that is, *without being caught*—it will go to you, Masters."

Jibril beamed, picking up Azril's explanation. With that, she tossed two syllables to Azril.

"You can join syllables to form a Word."

By way of example, Azril held up the two she'd received—*cher* and *kree*. As they whirled around her wrist, she explained:

"The meaning of your Word will materialize where you touch— whether it's a concept or an object or whatever."

""Ah!""

The moment they heard that, Sora and Shiro—saw the future. The two syllables from Azril's demonstration connected above her palm—and then—

"Nyaaaaaaaah, what's this?? It's gross—nyaaaaaaah!! Nyaaah!"

—a creature appeared, a giant *octopus*, wrapping her in its tentacles…materializing the future that Sora and Shiro had foreseen. Azril flailed about, screaming.

"My, my. You do know how to elicit the laughs, my elder—even going so far as to materialize words you are unable to read, as if you knew exactly what you were doing."

Jibril's cold smile seemed the least of Azril's concerns. Instantly— with a *thoom* of throbbing air—the Flügel blew away the octopus.

"L-like that, see?" said Azril, completely ignoring Sora's and

Shiro's squints. "The meaning of the completed Word materializes. Whether it's an object or a phenomenon or a concept, just as you imagine it."

"Note that because my elder was unable to read the syllables she joined, it was *my image that was materialized*, since I gave them to her. In the actual game, only you, Masters, will be able to use Words."

"……"

Jibril casually, unapologetically confessed that she had molested Azril. Yet Azril paid no mind as she cleared her throat and continued. "However—*each syllable will disappear after one use.* You'd better use them carefully, okay?"

—…

"This concludes the explanation, but do you have any questions, Masters?"

"Hell yeah, we do—*how are we supposed to run?* In case you don't know, humans can't fly."

"*Chatter chatter shiver shiver…*"

"…I do apologize, Master. By all rights I should be at your side—however, *it is not permitted for me to participate in this game.*"

To the two skeptical masters, Azril responded with a cackle.

"It wouldn't be a game if Jibs was on your side. No one would be able to catch you. At least I felt sorry enough for you to give you your Words. So let's do this—"

Brightening.

"You, the Dhampir hiding there—give 'em your wings." Azril turned.

—And that was enough to smash the stealth rite like glass, revealing Plum, who'd been hiding the whole time.

"…Hnh? Wha…huhhhhhhhh?! H-how'd you knowww?!"

"…Truly, I must say your lack of presence is remarkable."

—Jibril whispered admiringly at the companion whom even Sora and Shiro had been on the verge of forgetting.

Nearby, Azril smiled and asked Plum, "Hey, you. You may be a form of life lower than a mosquito, but surely you can weave a spell to make wings if you try hard enough to kill yourself?"

Azril dropped the question from a perch higher than a god's. Meanwhile, shivering in the fear of death, Plum plucked up the courage to answer.

"Uh, uhhhh? Th-there's no way I can make them fly at the speed of a Flügel... The shock wave alone would blow me to pieces, to say nothing of *them*... And anyway I'm just about out of—"

But Azril interrupted without breaking her smile—"When you get tired, you can just help yourself to their bodily fluids."

"On my honor! I shall work to weave wings with all of my heart!"

Betraying her principles at the speed of sound, Plum stood straight as an arrow and saluted. But—

"Hey, hold on here! Who says we even have to accept—?" Sora started to ask. But Jibril's demeanor cut him short.

—Please *do not despair of me.* And please *have faith in me*—

He considered the girl whose eyes conveyed an earnestness mixed with hope and unease, and next at her counterpart, whose smirk was like that of a corpse, empty and hollow.

"...Wish, and it shall be thine—if thou but kill its owner. That's how this game goes, 'kay?"

"......"

The nervous gaze of a soul, and the empty smile of a puppet. Sora saw in this challenge something he'd seen before, yet...

—*Game.* At this one word, Sora's and Shiro's eyes lit up, their heads rapidly cooling. Rules, conditions for victory, and even Azril's intentions fiercely assembled in their brains.

"...Brother."

Shiro, who had been doing the same thing, was nervous, but Sora nodded—*I know.*

—This was *clearly different* from the games they'd played before. A game was over before it began. This was " "'s creed, but now this—this was a game they'd been *coerced to accept.* A game they'd *not anticipated.* A game in which *the other side had the upper hand.* It was a game in which information lurked, hidden from them, exchanged in the tongue of Flügel. A game in which the rules had been unnaturally set so as to favor the Flügel. It was too dangerous. It was too suspicious. The information was too uncertain. There was no way they could be expected to accept this game.

"...Masters...I beg of you. *Please have faith in me.*"

But those eyes, wavering in anticipation of punishment yet conveying her heartfelt conviction of Sora and Shiro's victory, belonged to Jibril, *the one who had set up this game.*

"—Let us ask about certain conditions."

With a glance at his Flügel coconspirator, Sora muttered, his head cool as ice. Shiro had been looking up nervously, but now, if Sora had decided—Shiro cleared all worry from her expression and focused wholly on sharpening her thoughts. The siblings, aware that Jibril had closed her eyes in gratitude but not caring, crunched all manner of problems—to lay bare a game they'd not anticipated, to predict factors that couldn't conceivably be foreseen—and they revved their brains.

"—Shiro and I will be holding hands the whole time. That's one we can't budge on."

"...Those wings...Plum's making for us."

"Yeah. We require that we each have one wing and can move them as we wish."

"...Plum...*do it.*"

At Shiro's unreasonable abandonment of the courtesy of a question, Plum responded half crying.

"Uh, uuumm...? Th-that would take some really complex magic, so I'd like you to give me a break, if you—"

"We don't care how they look. In the meantime, we permit you to lick our sweat all you want."

"Leave it to meee!! I'll show you what a Dhampir is made ooof—nghh, rraghh!!"

With an unnecessarily fierce cry, Plum, her wings instantly stained bloodred, called up a complex pattern in her eyes. Weaving together an intricate rite, Plum transformed herself—

—into a scarf. She fluttered gently through the air, wrapping herself around Sora's and Shiro's necks with a *fwip*, connecting the pair in one long ascot.

"*Hff, hff...I disguised my presence in the physical...plane!* N-now... th-the ends of the scarf...sh-should work as wings. I think—!"

Much like she'd disguised herself as luggage when she first met Sora, Plum now assumed the form of a flying scarf. As even the Flügel looked on in wonder, Plum the Scarf gave the impression of sticking out her thin chest.

—Short of breath, the scarf that connected Sora and Shiro by the neck puffed out its ends. Seeing it trace an arterial pattern and weave itself into wings, Sora nodded. And then he raised the final issues.

"—And also...you have to transform the environment of Avant Heim so that it's totally feasible for Shiro, Plum, and me to function here. Plus, you say we're going to use her wings, but we don't know how. You need to give us a head start of—*five minutes* from the start of the game... Sound right to you, Shiro?"

"...Mm, that's fine."

—Everyone quietly gasped. Not because of the transfiguration of the two who, up to now, had been quivering heaps. No, it was their declaration that *five minutes* was all the head start they needed—that was why.

"That is—all right, isn't it?"

Jibril turned, putting the question to Azril and the nigh–one hundred Flügel assembled there. The Immanities would evade a hundred Flügel, employing a power they'd never used, with only forty-six syllables as their weapon. *If they really could do that*—everyone gulped.

"...Mm. All right. I do feel we're being a little easy on them, buuut..."

Azril, apparently alone in not getting it, groused but moved her finger slightly—whereupon there came a roar and a tremor.

"—Av'n's fulfilled your wish—so, shall we begin?"

Having nonchalantly reformed the environment of a world, Azril again snapped her fingers. Soundlessly, the wall deformed—opening a gigantic hole.

...Beyond the gaping hole in the wall, they could see the entirety of Avant Heim. Outside, whether Azril had moved everyone or it had simply been through the passage of time, night had fallen. With no sunlight, it was the perfect environment for Plum. Leaning out of the hole to check the atmosphere—Sora and Shiro squeezed their joined hands. They could guess that the scarf hanging from their necks—Plum—was struggling to stay silent as she flapped. They couldn't see what lay below them. Only the feeling that the onrushing wind would carry them away told them how high they were.

Behind Sora and Shiro, Jibril announced reverently, "Now—the game between my two masters and all the Flügel here shall commence presently."

Behind her, a hundred gazes. But—once Sora and Shiro were focused on a game, their thoughts were impenetrable.

"This is a map of Avant Heim."

Taking the paper as it fluttered in the wind, Shiro gave it a glance and nodded. Jibril took a step back and bowed her head deeply.

"...Masters, *thank you.*"

"I gotta say I'm worried, but...*I believe in you. You better not let me down.*"

"...*Family's* gotta be...protected...everyone knows that."

Jibril, Sora, and Shiro exchanged words only they understood, and then—

""—*Aschente*—!!""

All but Jibril raised their hands and shouted this. Sora and Shiro popped through the hole in the wall, into the open air. Immediately, gravity took hold. A force beyond human ability to fight. As the wind beat their faces, slowly—gradually—they accelerated downward. They couldn't see what was rushing up at them. But whatever it was, it could mean only one thing—death. Strangely bereft of all fear or concern— *Huh.* Sora chuckled to himself.

"...Brother..."

As Sora turned to look at his sister, the end of the scarf made a flapping noise—and opened into a wing. Confirming from his sister's expression that one like it was on his back—

"...Go...?"

Yeah—why would he be worried or afraid? Sora laughed. Holding hands tightly, flapping their wings, two in one. The mono-winged birds mightily defied gravity itself.

⏻ CHAPTER 2
ERROR

Meanwhile—Elkia Royal Castle, in the study of the previous king.

"……tuch. Stuch, I'm goddamn hungry, please."

Shaken gently, Steph felt her consciousness drifting up to the surface. Sprawled out on a desk, drooling, she rose with a start and looked around.

"—Wha…?! Uh, what, when did I fall asleep?!"

"After you ate, you banged your damn head on the desk, please. I thought you'd kicked the bucket, please."

Seems the moment her belly was filled, she'd passed out.

"Wh-what time is it…?" she inquired vacantly, folding up the coat that had been draped over her back—an act of kindness by Izuna, apparently. A cute *grmbrbrbrrrrl* sound answered her. Izuna laced her hands over her stomach, entreating Steph sincerely.

"Exactly six hours since food, please."

"…Y-you certainly keep a precise clock."

They'd last eaten at about two AM, if memory served—so it had to be morning? The young sun was unable to shine its rays into the windowless study, but by now, the town would be getting active.

"Stuch. Stuch, food, please."

As the Werebeast tugged insistently at her clothes, Steph acquiesced. "Ahh... Yes, I suppose so... All right, I'll make some breakfast... Wait, what's that?"

Suddenly, Steph noticed the mountain of books stacked where Izuna had been sitting.

"Miss Izuna, what is that?"

"...? Books, please?"

"No, I mean—why are they there?"

"...Obviously 'cos I read 'em, please?"

"—What? Since when do you know how to read...?!"

"I told you I'd learn your damn script, please. So I *learned it*, please."

Impossible—Steph's eyes popped. The matching game Steph had given Izuna that used Werebeast and Immanity script—the book for learning the Werebeast tongue. Just with that, in the time Steph had been unconscious, Izuna had learned Immanity's language and read that many books—?

—Anything other than games was beyond Steph. But so long as it was a game— Seeing how Izuna had proven her prowess in an instant and already read more books than she had herself, Steph's hair stood on end.

"......No wonder you get along so well with Sora and Shiro."

Steph was struck by a fact that Sora and Shiro usually overshadowed. This small child, Izuna Hatsuse. This Werebeast girl, even younger than Shiro—who'd brought a match with " ", of all opponents, to within a hairbreadth—was, without a doubt, *the real thing*. But...

"...Miss Izuna, when was the last time you slept?"

"...Huh? I-I've had five meals...so, uh...please."

Trying to count on her fingers, Izuna's face darkened. Shadowy circles under her eyes evidenced that it had been long since she'd slept a wink.

If you thought about it, it made sense. However much one might be the real thing, *it wasn't as if anything could be accomplished without effort.* Izuna had given her all, foregoing sleep entirely—just to learn Immanity and read all these books.

"...I'm sorry, Miss Izuna. I slept while you..."

"You're such a wuss, please. Small fries should know to sleep when they get tired, please."

Steph grinned at Izuna's bluster. Seeing a faint ray of hope in the endless toil, she drummed herself up and slapped her cheeks. First, she'd make some food, and then— But as she turned to leave the study—

"...? Miss Izuna, in what order are you reading these books?"

—she noticed that the tomes had been extracted *in a deliberate fashion* from the various shelves.

"Starting with the ones that *smell good*, please."

It was a cryptic answer, yet Izuna spoke as if it was obvious. Noticing the title of the book atop the stack, Steph picked it up. Indeed—it was related to the place Sora and Shiro found themselves.

Steph read the title, written in the hand of the previous king—her grandfather—aloud: "—*Flügel: A Weapon without a Master*...What made you pick this one?"

Izuna sniffed the book. "Damn thing smelled like Sora and Shiro, please. Guess they read it about a month ago, please?"

"They read it...?"

—At the beach, after they'd returned from Oceand, Sora had casually declared that they'd bust into Avant Heim and get three races. Steph, having been told nothing of how it was to be done—not like that was anything new—opened the book. A month ago. That would mean they'd read it before playing the Eastern Union... She skimmed the contents, lined up in letters directly set down by her grandfather, like all the books in this room.

Flügel—a god-slaying race created by Artosh, god of war, in the ancient Great War—

* * *

Flügel—these heavenly women collect knowledge not for amusement. This was what the previous king—her grandfather—had written about the Flügel based on his observations. In other words, it was his insight into Jibril. Presumably... But. *They do it to live— Nay. To not die.* The inscrutable Jibril floated in the back of Steph's mind. *They are living weapons having lost their master...lifeless puppets only wandering, hollow.* She visualized that girl, with her unreadable smile and ridiculous devotion to her curiosity and her masters. *Where is their reason to live—nay, the proof that they are even alive?* —What was it? The Jibril described by her grandfather didn't remotely match the Jibril she knew. Disquieted by this disparity, Steph unconsciously stopped turning the pages and thought.

...Sora and Shiro had read this before venturing to Avant Heim. Just what were they—?

"Stuch, we don't have time for you to be sitting here reading that shit, please."

"Uh, oh, y-yes, you're right."

That was right. Their task wasn't to research Flügel, but Siren— Steph reoriented herself, only to be interrupted by another *grm-brbrbrbrrrrrl.*

"It's time for food, please," Izuna declared with those decisive, round eyes.

Steph grinned wryly and went to return the book to its shelf when—it must have been from overwork—she went dizzy. "Oh..."

The books tumbled from the shelf she'd grabbed to steady herself. As read and unread books intermingled—and she felt ready to break down into pitiful wailing—

—a wind blew past at a speed too quick for Steph to react to. It was all she could do just to recognize the blur. Izuna had moved from the door to the corner in an instant—and now held a book in her mouth.

"...? What's this shit, please?"

"...Th-that's what I want to know. What in the world is this about?"

Ignoring Steph and her obvious confusion, Izuna sniffed the book suspiciously.

"Smells like fish, please...? No, please... Oh."

Then, flinging the album aside as if it was of no interest, she said:

"Smells like Siren, please. Can't eat those bitches, please."

——Instantly, amidst Steph's hazy thoughts, a light shone. Just now, when she'd asked Izuna in what order she was selecting books, she'd said starting with the ones that *smelled good*. How had she been able to tell that Sora and Shiro had read—? No, more critically:

"Wh-why does a book of my grandfather's smell like Siren?!"

"Dunno, please. Either a Siren touched it or someone who touched a Siren touched it, please," replied Izuna, cocking her head.

"Like Sora or Shiro...or you or me?!"

"...? No, please. It's just got the same geezer smell mixed in as all these books, please."

It wasn't their scent. Not Sora's or Shiro's. For starters, as far as she knew, they hadn't come here since Oceand—so—?!

"C-can you tell when it was touched?"

While Steph fell over herself asking, Izuna counted her fingers, frowning, and then answered: "...Don't have enough fingers, please."

That was all but confirmation that it was from over ten years ago.

"...W-wait just a moment. You can tell that?"

"You can't, please? Damn smell doesn't run away, please."

How am I supposed to know the common sense of another race?, Steph screamed inwardly, yet now—all the riddles were answered. The point of having Izuna help her, the method by which she'd identified books Sora and Shiro had read—and the fact that her grandfather had been involved with the Sirens over ten years ago... Everything had been laid bare! Now all that was left...!

"C-can you distinguish between books that were written before and after this one?!"

Izuna sniffed and tilted her head.

"...Smell's weak, please. But if I try *damn hard...should be possible*, please."

—The world filled with light. The scope of their search had narrowed tremendously!

"Ohhhhh, if you had such a useful power, I wish you would have employed it soooooner, but thank you so muuuuch. Finally, I've glimpsed a way out of this—"

Overcome with emotion, Steph hugged Izuna and rubbed her all over. But Izuna jumped back.

"—*Hhhhh!!*"

She threatened Steph as if about to bite her, her hair on end.

"Eh, u-umm...I-I apologize. Did I offend you?"

"...Stuch, you suck at petting, please!"

As Izuna maintained her defensive posture, Steph looked around in a panic. What caught her eye—

"Oh, y-yes. H-here, you can have this. Will you forgive me?"

"—The hell's that, please?"

"I-it's a confection I prepared for myself. S-see?"

Eating a piece herself to demonstrate that it was safe—she shakily proffered the goods. As she extended her peace offering, Izuna sniffed it several times.

"......Not bad, please. But right now I want food, please. Fish, please."

—Snapping up the confection in her mouth, Izuna immediately recovered her good humor. Waving her big tail to and fro, she nibbled at the sweet snack like a hamster.

"Ah, w-well, I'll go cook! Grilled fish, boiled fish, raw fish... which—?"

"All of them, please."

"Wha—?"

"*All* of them, please."

"Why not! Now that I have found an ally to be reckoned with, why not display my true potential in the kitchen with every seafood dish in my repertoire!! In the meantime, could you segregate the books

that my grandfather wrote before and after?!" Steph addressed a rapt fountain of drool.

"Understood, please!"

Izuna bolted up in time with her loud and clear response.

At last, the way out was in sight! Just as Steph started to fly out of the room, behind her—

—something *broke* with a bang.

"I'm sorry?"

Only when the Werebeast—growling, heart pounding as if about to leap out of her chest, panting, with close to ten books in her hands, stained scarlet by her bloodbreak—prodded her for action, did Steph realize the sound had been Izuna *breaking the sound barrier.*

"...—*Hh, hff*— I'm done, please—! Where's my fish, please?!"

...If I try damn hard...should be possible. Well, well. Exactly as Izuna had promised, she'd tried damn hard.

—She'd tried so hard, she'd picked a fight with the limits of physics and bent them by force...

Izuna's blood raged, her drool dripped, her gaze fixed as if on prey—

"...W-would you mind helping me buy some groceries?"

Steph decided to buy time...

—High in the sky of Avant Heim, enshrouded in the dark of night. The landscape was littered with countless cubes and lit only by the moon and the faint glow emitted by the cubes themselves. It was through all this that Sora and Shiro awkwardly, shakily, unconvincingly flew—or drifted.

"U-umm... Do you *really* have a chance of winning...?"

"Don't talk to me now—you're distracting me!"

"...Brother...more...more like this..."

They looked as if one false move would plummet them into a tailspin, which was not very reassuring at all.

Plum, who connected them through formed wings, murmured,

"Y-you're playing against *Flügel*, you know. I mean, you may have my help, but *still*, it's not as if you've ever flown *before*... And there's no way we can win on speed against *Flügel*..."

Struggling with the use of his wing, Sora answered merrily, if only in terms of his tone:

"Don't...worry. Being fast is an advantage in tag—but it doesn't necessarily mean you'll win."

"Well, that's true...but still..."

At this stage, Plum the Scarf heaved a silent sigh.

—Flügel. Even if they couldn't shift, they were a race that contravened physics by their very existence. The trio might never have seen their opponents' top speed, but knowing their general nature was enough to imagine it. Probably, if they really tried—one might not be talking supersonic, more like hypersonic. Even allowing that tag wasn't just about raw speed, there was no way you could expect a tortoise to beat a horse in a race. Seriously, the way they were going—it was—totally—?

"...Huh? Wh-what?"

Amidst these thoughts, Plum caught on to something funny. At some point, Sora and Shiro's flapping had stabilized. Gradually, their pace increased, and the wind beating against the muffler—Plum—grew stronger.

"...Uumm, why did you have to make it so each of you—control just one wing?"

Thinking of this at such a late hour didn't stop Plum from asking the question. The siblings, who were making the wings their own in the blink of an eye, looked at each other and smiled.

"That's obvious—'cos if we didn't, we couldn't be sure we'd win."

Suggesting, conversely, that *if they did, they could be sure they'd win*, their joined hands told the story.

—As long as our hands are touching.

——We're not gonna lose to anyone.

■■■

Empty weapons—objects…mere puppets—Flügel. Tools to destroy gods for their lord. This was enough for them. But it had been six thousand–odd years since they had lost their lord. Why did Flügel still exist? In search of this Answer, they had long drifted along with Avant Heim. But Jibril—who had flown off on her own and now suddenly returned—had clearly changed. As if, yes—she'd found the Answer.

…

Azril, chin in hand, looked up into the empty space. As per Sora and Shiro's conditions, the entire assemblage of the hall—a hundred Flügel—waited out the siblings' five-minute head start, all gazing in the same direction. At the image projected in the empty space—Sora and Shiro's exploits.

"…Jibs, I think if any kid can complete the final mission Lord Artosh left us—to find the Answer—it can be only you, Jibs, the Closing Number."

"……"

—There was a reason for this. But that wasn't the issue, Azril decided as she continued.

"If your Answer is one planted in you by the Covenants—"

—Something Azril had confirmed, *in the Flügel tongue* so as not to be understood by Sora and Shiro… She went on deliberately, her plastic smile unchanged.

"—I'll use my 'privilege.' You know what that means, don't you?"

"Yes. However—to ask a question without already knowing the answer is the work of a weak will, my elder."

At these words, all the Flügel staring up at the display stiffened.

—Azril, the Alipotentiary—the chair of the Council of Eighteen Wings. The one privilege held by Azril, who was not the agent plenipotentiary, was based on an agreement struck six thousand–odd years earlier.

"—*The order for all Flügel to end themselves*…is this not what you mean?" Jibril narrowed her eyes as she casually voiced what everyone was thinking. "Originally, this was a privilege you secured in order to prohibit our suicide until we might find the meaning of our existence as Flügel without a lord. Should you, however, *judge there to be no meaning to our existence*—please feel free."

What tensed in all of them was not fear—Flügel had never held a strong fear of death. For a race created as weapons, a race that lived eternally, it was almost an honor. What took hold inside them despite this was anticipation.

—Something starting or something ending. Just that difference. But the promise of such an event created an atmosphere of anticipation.

"...As long as you...know."

But it appeared that, alone among them, only Azril failed to grasp this. Considering her elder, Jibril could not help but evince a slight disappointment.

—And that, more than anything, gnawed at Azril.

"Elder Azril. Surely you can understand it as well. Our—Flügel's—*fundamental mistake.*"

—Sora and Shiro didn't know, but Jibril, since meeting them—*had clearly changed.* Before losing to them, Jibril too might have felt some unease as she moved through her days. When it came down to it, though, she'd been more or less the same as Azril. Turning the unknown into the known—in that alone, she'd found meaning. The unknown was to be overturned. It was unemotional, or—one might even say—an enemy to be destroyed. Jibril had just been a little more aggressive than the others in confronting that enemy.

—But the day she lost to Sora and Shiro, that changed.

"The knowledge we have accumulated over the course of thousands—tens of thousands—of years is upended in its whole by my masters, born scarcely over ten years ago. The meaning, the value of that—my elder, you do not understand."

"......"

With an expression Azril had never seen, almost feverish—an expression that, as far as memory served, her little sister had never shown even to Artosh—Jibril elaborated.

"The heart burns when the unknown is transformed into the known. Hotter by far, though—*when the known is transformed into the unknown*. This revelation convinced me, of my own will, to follow. It has nothing to do with the Covenants."

Azril could only look on in silence during Jibril's oration. Frankly speaking, she had no idea what her little sister was talking about. The known transformed into the unknown—? What could that mean but terror?

—But as if inspired by Jibril's words, heat welled in the eyes of the hundred Flügel raring at the starting line—and their wings quivered.

I don't get this, Azril seemed to say as she put her chin back in her hand. At the very least—it wasn't the Answer. She turned her attention to the two projected in the air—awkwardly struggling to fly.

"Elder Azril, I know that you, more than anyone else, have anguished over the fate of the Flügel. However."

"......"

Otherwise unmoving, Azril flicked her eyes toward the remark, where her gaze was met with—absolute conviction.

—Somehow, as if pleading, Jibril spoke.

"The answer you have been seeking is not where you imagine."

■■■

"Eegh...eegh...I-I can't *take* anymore... It's too hard... I give up..."

"Dude, it hasn't even been three minutes! Even Ul*raman has more guts than you!"

Plum the Scarf was already whining and getting upbraided by Sora.

"I'm not some crazy Flügel! You two don't even know how hard it is for me to defy gravityyy! And then you want me to give you wings. To be honest, I wish you'd—"

"You want sweat? I got plenty, so lick it all you want!"

"I'll never give uuup!! For your sweat—come, let us continue!"

"Damn, you make yourself look ridiculous!!"

.The sensation of having his neck licked sent something unpleasant screaming down Sora's spine.

—This scarf was supposed to be Plum incognito. She had cloaked her physical self in the form of a scarf to link Sora and Shiro, with her "ends" functioning as wings that the siblings could manipulate at will. That was how it worked. It was a disguise, which meant it was a spell of illusion. So—Sora reminded himself that it was actually just Plum.

"Hey. To us, it looks like you're a scarf that turns into wings. But what's the real situation?"

"*Lickety-lickety...* Ohh, this is heaven. ♥ Oh, yes? Umm, well, at the moment, I am holding you by your neck while licking it, you seee...while I am latched on to Queen Shiro's neck with my lower extremitieees."

"Ha-ha, let's call this flying in 'deformation'!"

"...Brother, that is lame, obnoxious, and, most of all...not funny..."

"Hey, I just gave it a shot. Why you gotta be like that?!"

A tear fell, sparkling through the night sky of Avant Heim. But Plum chimed in bitterly.

"Just so you *know*, simultaneous deployment of multiple rites is Elf's patented specialty. Considering I'm not only disguising myself as a magical flying scarf, but also magically flying you through the air however you want, I really—*reaaaaaaaaaaaaaaally!*—wish you'd say something nice!!"

Plum complained at *length*.

"Also, this tires me out more than I expected... If my soul supply cuts out, we'll probably die in a few secooonds."

"...You sure jumped in on a pretty risky proposal, didn't you?"

"Uh, but then I get to lickety-lickety your neck all I want, Sir... Gee-hee-heee, it's so delectable!"

"Nggahh! Now I just want to whip off this damn scarf!"

Just as the impulse struck him to toss the scarf, regardless of the consequences—

*   *   *

"...Brother, time."

Five minutes had passed. Sora's eyes narrowed at Shiro's reminder. It was the time for the Flügel held at the starting line to come hunt them down.

"—All right, Plum, we're trusting you with our lives, so don't crap out on us in the middle."

"Not to worry! If I run out of energy, we'll just go down togetherrr!"

"That's nice, but no thanks!! Here we go!"

The moment he said it, Sora and Shiro simultaneously flapped hard—reducing their altitude precipitously.

"Eeeyhyaaghh!"

The plunge was so steep that even Plum, still wrapped around their necks, screamed. Amplified by the force of their wings, their downward velocity was so intense that the wind beat against them. Just before they hit the ground—Avant Heim's back—they leveled off into horizontal flight.

Are they...using the acceleration from the fall to leave their pursuers behind? Plum silently wondered, *but—* Something was behind them. The Flügel, who had just started, were already catching up. It was true that Sora and Shiro had gotten the hang of their wings quickly. But no matter how hard they pushed the wings Plum had woven for them, they couldn't surpass the limits of physics. Two hundred kilometers per hour was the best they could hope for, whereas Flügel scoffed at physics. *Th-they're about to catch up to us! What do we do?!* While Plum wailed internally, Sora and Shiro calmly assessed the situation behind them—

"Four. No formation."

"...*Syllables*: one, three..."

"Evade. Collect?"

"...Number One, wing base: *oh*...Three, left side: *hol.*"

"One: Shiro. Three: me. Go."

—An exchange indecipherable to Plum transpired in a blink, and before Plum could so much as mumble, *Huh?*—Sora and Shiro tweaked their course.

—That instant.

"Eh-heh-hehh! I'm first!"

"We have you now!"

Making short work of the five-minute handicap as might be expected, two Flügel closed in. They reached out toward Sora and Shiro—but grasped empty air.

""—Wh-what?""

The two Flügel, voicing their incomprehension at having failed to snatch the siblings, who'd vanished in a blink—

""Uhh!""

Behind. Sora and Shiro were, respectively, on their assailants' *wing base and left side*—targeting the syllables transcribed there—and the Flügel moaned. The other two, who followed a moment later, looked around, having lost sight of their prey. It was no wonder, for by then Sora and Shiro were well on their *spiraling path* through the lines of cubes. Weaving among countless stacks of die—through the townscape of Avant Heim.

—Two syllables in hand.

"...Uh, excuse me...what was...?!"

A fleeting encounter that defied even Plum's comprehension, and she was wrapped around their necks. As Plum gaped behind the spell of her illusion, Sora filled her in.

"A *barrel roll*—that's how you dodge something flying in a straight line faster than you, duh."

—Indeed, feeling pursuers at their backs and drawing them in as close as possible, Sora and Shiro had tweaked their course so that, of the four on their tail—the two bearing syllables would *wind up in front of them*. And the instant Sora and Shiro seized what they needed, they stuck out their wings and just *rolled off at an angle*. That meant they kept going in the same direction, but in a decelerating spiral. While, from the relative perspective of the too-fast Flügel, it seemed they'd vanished in midair—really, the siblings had just "outstripped" them. They weren't used to using wings, and even if they mastered them, they were incapable of Flügel speed. In which case—

"If we can't work our wings, we can just *stop them*. Those bitches fly around all 'Screw aerodynamics'—like they know the maneuvers of fixed-wing aircraft."

"...Even if they know...they'd never have...thought about it."

Around the arms of the smugly smiling pair, just as Shiro had explained—revolved the syllables *oh* and *hol*. Plum, finally catching up, was dumbfounded.

"...Don't tell me...you remember *everyone who has a syllable—and which ones*?!"

Sora chuckled.

"Come on, Plum, you still haven't learned to respect my little sister?"

Feeling shamed by these simple words, Plum fell silent.

"Well, in any case...Shiro, the syllables we need right now—you know, right?"

"...Naturally."

"'Kay, then we'll *catch* those first. It's not like we can keep using the same maneuvers on these guys, after all."

"...Mm, roger that..."

—Plum gaped at the pair casually declaring that they'd *catch* Flügel, as if such a thing were natural. It was as if they had decided that in this game of tag, the siblings were actually "it." Sora and Shiro soared through the cityscape of Avant Heim, weaving as they went.

■■■

—Alone at the starting line with Azril, watching the scene projected before them, Jibril felt a flutter in her chest—a fervent sense of astonishment. At Shiro, who remembered all the syllables, their bearers, and even where they'd been transcribed. At their divine feat of evasion and the collection of the syllables—but, *more than that*, at her two lords flying about the city as if they knew it like their own backyard. She could not conceal her astonishment.

Avant Heim was constructed of intricately overlapping cubes. Through the fine cracks between the cubes, in the darkness illuminated only by the faint light and the moon, they flew as if threading needles. They still had little by way of speed. But in this scenario, a pursuer who *flew too quickly would be lost*. As they soared, diving, piercing precisely through the narrow alleys and cracks formed by the cubes, slipping through holes it seemed hard to imagine that even *one* person could fit through, one careless acceleration—would result in a calamitous crash.

...*What magnificence... But still*, that left something unexplained. Jibril puzzled to herself. Flügel was a race that tended to rely on brute strength. This was a truism she herself could not deny. But even so, they did know how to collaborate. They wouldn't be much of a weapon otherwise. If speed was insufficient, they should switch to siege tactics—and yet—

"Huh—what?! Wha...? How—?!"

A Flügel girl shrieked. She'd been poised at the only exit from the crack into which Sora and Shiro had ducked—only to watch them burst from someplace completely unexpected.

Yes, Sora and Shiro had foiled the Flügel siege entirely. They'd glanced at the map for only a moment. Had they learned everything about Avant Heim in that short time?

—Impossible. It was conceivable that one of her masters—Shiro—could have memorized a map in those few seconds. But it was impossible to divine the cracks and alleys of the city, built by complex, three-dimensional stacks of bodies high and low, from a mere map. *Then how...?* And at last, careful observer that she was, Jibril nevertheless doubted the conclusion that she, of all people, had reached.

■■■

...*Wha—? Th-this is a joke, righhht?*

—Realization dawned that between Sora's and Shiro's firmly joined hands—their fingers were *finely moving*. Plum, who until recently had been desperately suppressing a cry, now believing that she had discovered the methodology by which her pilots were navigating implausibly narrow holes and cracks—a methodology one might safely dub "bullshitology"—suddenly found herself speechless.

So, probably…presumably…not that it was plausible—this is how they did it. Skimming the cityscape that Shiro had memorized, she confirmed that the cubes' sizes were uniform. Through mental calculation, she then unraveled the patterns by which those cubes were stacked, revealing fine cracks that arose based on differences in level. Bypassing the necessity for words, she conveyed this information to Sora through finger movement alone, and Sora, in turn, shook their pursuers by deceiving them, leading them on, and plotting out escape routes.

—How could one find themselves at anything but a loss for words? As far as Plum was concerned (and pretty much anyone would agree), it was totally beyond all comprehension. They were communicating by finger movement. Yet simple information like "This way" or "Over there" *wasn't even what it was.* Reading each other's intentions from the sensation of their joined hands, the two Immanities, without a moment's confusion or hesitation, flapped their wings and flew as if their connected palms were their very nerves. Well, it was fair to say that they had not yet completely acclimated themselves to flight. There was still some roughness in their execution. But all the more for that—witnessing something beyond belief—Plum was astonished.

Two in one set of wings—holding hands. If one twin worked harder to break gravity's pull, the other would sense that effort *before they were left behind,* match it, and catch up. Without allowing a single flap of the wings to fall out of sync, *they shared with one another what they learned and raised each other up.*

—Limitlessly. At terrifying speed. The sight sent a shiver down Plum's spine. These two—were even more—

—Then the siblings, who up to that point had maintained radio silence, opened their mouths.

"Left, right: four, four drawn."

"...Left: *shal, yoo, pahs, sel.* Right: *reyt, er, not, roh. Missing one.*"

"Collect, draw above. Twelve?"

"...Syllables: five. *Completes...but risky.*"

Following this cryptic exchange, a smiling Sora resumed speaking in complete sentences.

"Risk acknowledged—! *Let's get 'em!!*"

"...Roger! Left Shiro, brother right. Left shoulder, right wing, left elbow, hip!"

No sooner had they spoken—

"Eeyahhhhh!!"

They snapped their wings—that is, Plum—in a vicious break that sent them hurtling into a narrow hole...

"—! We have them at last!"

"Pincer attack, on cue!"

Sora and Shiro carelessly—or so it seemed to Plum—exited into a wide corridor. Waiting for them were four Flügel on either side—as they'd said themselves, a perfect pincer attack. But Sora's and Shiro's words echoed through Plum's head.

—*Left, right: four, four drawn...*they'd drawn the Flügel—and now they'd *get them?* Rushing forward with blinding speed, eight Flügel in total to their left and right, but in that case—

"Let's do it, Shiro!!"

"...Mm!"

—*Just who had who?*— Sora and Shiro brought together their free hands to form a Word. The syllables on their wrists moved and combined—a flash of light. Targeting the eight Flügel assaulting them from either flank, the pair—held their hands out left and right and shouted:

""—'Hollow!'""

—A heartbeat. The four Flügel from each side descending on Sora and Shiro with outstretched hands—

""...Huh?""

—only to pass harmlessly through their prey, reemerging on opposite sides.

""Waungh!""

Leaving eight moans in their wake, Sora and Shiro dove once more into the space between cubes. Navigating a crevice barely wide enough for one person, aligned vertically with Shiro, Sora laughed.

"*Pahs, sel, yoo, shal*—how 'bout it, Shiro? I got 'em all!"

"...*Reyt, roh, not, er*... That makes eight..."

Each displayed the four syllables of light they had collected on their wrists, as if it was only natural.

—Gingerly, Plum inquired:

"...Uh, excuse me...what was...?"

"What do you think? A hole. 'Words' work on whatever you touch—those are the rules of the game, right?"

"...So...we opened a hole...in space."

Plum, speechless, thought back. They'd opened a hole—a hollow space—around themselves, bridging the space at their flanks to evade the Flügel's pincer attack. Once their assailants emerged, naturally, their backs would be to Sora and Shiro—who collected the syllables—but wait.

"...Could it be you *drew in only Flügel with syllablesss*?!"

"Yeah, but we didn't get all the ones we need—"

Affirming this as if it was nothing, Sora looked up audaciously from the syllables lined up on his arm like prayer beads.

—Plum involuntarily followed his gaze.

...Four, five, eight—twelve Flügel were converging on them at terrifying speed.

"Ah-wah-wah-wah-wah-wah-wah—what are we going to dooo?!"

"*Collect. Draw twelve from above*—just like we planned. Don't freak out."

"...Brother, can we get out?"

Sora and Shiro were barreling at high velocity through a crack barely big enough for one person. As soon as they shot into the open again, they'd be assaulted by Flügel—twelve of them. But Sora grinned boldly—

"Sure, no prrrrrob—!"

Sora lost his balance as Plum suddenly licked his neck. They burst into the open—with twelve Flügel incoming. With Sora off-kilter, the centrifugal force—

"…Brother?!"

"Wwwaaaaah?!"

—almost bucked Shiro, but some furious wing flapping just managed to keep them whole. Even so, the effort to avoid a tailspin left Sora unprepared for the Flügel rushing in.

"——Shiro, do iiit!"

—A split-second decision. No time to right themselves. Sora extended his left hand to Shiro—and left the Word to her, wholly convinced she'd know what he meant. Shiro grabbed Sora's hand and pushed the glowing syllables out into the void—

"—'You shall not pass'…!"

With these words, the twelve onrushing shadows descended on Sora and Shiro, and…

"Owwiee!"

"Ngyah!"

Whap, whap, whap—no, not even so half-assed and meekly. Thunderously, like a shelter being bombarded, the Flügel pounded into an invisible wall. But the real issue was—! Shiro glanced at Sora. They'd *planned*—to break upward at this point.

—"You shall not pass." The wall they'd constructed using four separate monosyllabic words—*let no enemy pass*. Their plan had been to snare just the Flügel with syllables slipping by, but…

"Ngk—! Rraghh!"

—He was in time. Shiro's expression relaxed. While he'd let Shiro launch the Word, her brother had managed to regain his balance and flip over. Breaking out in a nervous sweat, Sora flapped his wing as Shiro simultaneously followed his lead—! Weaving past the twelve Flügel momentarily stunned by their impact with the invisible wall—

"Shit, Shiro—do it for me!"

"—Mm!"

There was no time to relay which of their assailants had syllables. Shiro stretched out her hands—and then... Hands alone being insufficient, she employed her feet—and even her wing, barely managing to collect them all.

"Mgmgmgggg, we won't let you get—"

"I won't let you do that!!"

Shiro's wing was on the verge of getting tagged, but this time Sora used *his* wing to adjust *their mutual* balance. They scraped by past the hands of the fiends, slipping back under the invisible wall... and, just as they were about to crash into the ground, they flapped off—ducking into a narrow crack... They'd made it somehow.

"...*Hff*...*hff!*"

Shiro voiced her concern for Sora as he struggled to catch his breath.

"U-umm... Are you all right?" queried Plum as well, herself the culprit of this crisis.

Sora chewed on the scarf and howled indistinctly. "—Pluuuuuum! You little shit, you really wanna die with us?!"

"I-I-I'm sorry! You see, when you made that sharp turn, my mouth slipped off you, Sir— Did I not tell you that if my supply were cut off we would die in a matter of secooonds?! I mean, if we die, we'll die together. You'll be coming with meee!!"

—That twerp. She had some damn nerve. With that, Shiro suppressed the pounding of her heart to catalog the syllables at her wrist and mumbled:

"...Brother...we got...*ak, por, bair, vey, feet, teyt,* and *dih*—now..."

"Yeah, *it's finally complete.*"

Por, dih, sel, er, vey, bair, roh, reyt, ak, feet, and *teyt*—the siblings smiled at the Word they could now compile. As they locked eyes and nodded—they flapped their wings hard. The two, who had thus far kept to weaving among the cubes, now ascended to the sky.

"—Oh, there!"

"Mmk...they're changing their strategy again?"

They were spotted immediately. Sora and Shiro exposed themselves, but their pursuers were suspicious of this sudden appearance.

Rather than attacking in straight lines, they flew in arcs to close in and surround their quarry.

—No one could have predicted it. Even Plum, despite everything, hadn't seen it coming. Before the advancing Flügel, the two joined hands and spelled out the Word.

—Before the four syllables faded, *they touched themselves* and shouted:

""—'Accelerate!'""

■■■

It wasn't just their pursuers. Plum and even Jibril observing from afar were dumbfounded. Who would have expected that, in the short time since obtaining their wings at the start of the game—not even fifteen minutes—those same wings borrowed from Plum would, with a single flap from two Immanities…

…leave both sound and Flügel far behind with nothing but a shock wave in their wake, using straight-up *linear distance*.

Indeed, using a Word to accelerate themselves, they could materialize an image. Then they could get rid of their wings' physical limitations. *"Hasten," "agility," "accelerate"*—since the start of the game, their goal had been to form such Words. Failing to do so, Sora and Shiro would have been incapable of escaping adversaries who changed strategies according to their opponents' movements—who adapted and learned—for a full hour. That's why they'd stuck to low speeds around the cubes, focused on drawing in Flügel and collecting syllables. Now Jibril saw this, and she squinted as if peering into bright light.

—Because *this proved they had faith in Flügel.*

"Ha-ha! This is fun!"

"…Mm-hm!"

As the two rolled as if dancing in midair, their laughs resounded through Avant Heim.

—*Two wings, one fate*: The idiom crossed Jibril's mind. But—even that was not right, she felt as she shook her head. What she was witnessing was not "two wings, one fate" in the figurative sense of being very close. It was the two one-winged birds of the expression's original, literal meaning, she was sure. A male and a female, each with one eye and one wing, who always flew together. These fantastic animals—

—are flying before us at this very moment, are they not?

Jibril stared at them as if dazzled—but.

"......"

Azril, looking on, bored, still did not grasp *what it meant.*

—Seeing this, Jibril inquired quietly:

"Elder, do you know the reason I opposed the Sharing Act?"

"...Because you're too serious and don't like others touching your stuff?"

"No. It is because I enjoy—reading the same books many times."

—That was news. Azril considered her questioningly.

"...What for? *Who needs them once you've memorized them?*"

"Yes, I knew this is what you would say, and that is why I had not spoken of it..."

Jibril sighed and then, apparently steeling herself, said:

"Even after one has read a book, when one returns after learning more outside it, there are new discoveries to be found."

"......"

"What bothered me was being unable to read them whenever I wanted. Do you not see?"

"...See what?"

"—If you only memorize the contents, *it ends there.*"

Jibril lowered her eyes at this statement—yet.

—Azril still seemed confused. Not comprehending Jibril's insight, yes, but more critically—

"——So what does that have to do with this?"

...

...The look Jibril gave her was terribly pained. It was not a look of scorn or derision. It was a look, rather, of disappointment, of falling deeper and deeper every time a faint hope was once again cut down.

—Azril couldn't answer her sister's hopes. That, more than anything else, stabbed her keenly.

"What are you saying...? What's the problem...?!"

■■■

High in the night sky of Avant Heim rushed a silver trail. Sora and Shiro had already left the sound barrier far behind—by now there was no one who could catch up.

"Well, as long as we don't let our guard down, we're pretty much safe from getting caught."

Sora muttered this as he held hands with Shiro and burst through the night sky, yet—

"...But what about...the syllables...?"

"Yeah, I know. If we're gonna play this game, we ought to *beat it with a full collection of syllables*. Plus"—nodding at Shiro's words, Sora pulled his expression together—"I already know the Word I want to shoot into *her*."

"'Her'...? Of whom do you speaaak?"

Plum asked, but Sora didn't answer. He just turned his back.

It was nice they'd lost them with their speed—but to collect the syllables, they'd have to get close. Which meant a risk of getting caught, and on top of that, they were facing Flügel. Also—

Sora admonished himself internally.

—Don't forget: This game was unexpected. "   " didn't have the home-field advantage. No matter how mindful they were of risks, there was no way they could guard against everything.

"...Ha, interesting."

Sora chuckled, unheard. Excellent—this was what made it worth playing! So they'd have to minimize the risks—by *collecting as many syllables as possible at once*. If they buffed up their insurance, that is, the power of Words, they'd be in a better position... But then Sora looked back to see—

—a gleaming ray.

"...Uh?"

Shiro raised a questioning voice at the light.

"—Eeerk?!"

Sora responded a fraction of a second faster to precisely what he'd just been anticipating. He swung himself down—breaking out their axis into a curving roll without changing their course—

"E-excuse me, what are you—ngyaaaah?!"

Cutting Plum short, a flash shot past—*along their former axis.*

—It had been a split-second decision. The incredible evasive action encouraged Shiro to praise her brother, but before she could...

"Jibriiiiil!! The hell was that? We didn't hear about this! *They can attack us?!*"

...Sora, previously so composed, was now shouting furiously. Above his head—*poonk.* A little Jibril, her head about a quarter of her height, appeared and announced:

"No, Master. That was not an attack. It was a homing capture spell."

"Don't you mean a missile?!"

"No, it is perfectly nonlethal. The spell merely serves to bind the target and pull it in. Considering this and its purpose of capture rather than destruction, its concept is quite different from that of a 'missile' in your—"

Tearing his hair in response to Jibril's cluelessness, Sora howled.

"Okay, I'll rephrase that. We didn't hear anything about *projectiles*! Can't we fire back, Plum?!"

"Please don't talk crazyyy! I said duocasting is Elf's patented specialtyyy. If I use any more magic than this, I'll shrivel uuup! Never mind that your neck has already turned into a wrinkly mess, Sir!!"

"So what if it's wrinkly?! You want some *cold sweat*? I've got a shit-ton down my back by now, so lick it up!"

"Really?! Don't mind if I dooo! Ahh! ♥"

With an irritated tongue-click at Plum, who seamlessly switched tracks from weepy to happy voice, Sora looked back. It's an away game, so be ready for anything—that's what he'd been thinking, and now look! Sure, the Flügel had said that there would be no shifting—but.

—No one ever said there wouldn't be any magic—!

"—Damn it—how could I miss that?"

"…Should have thought, of it…!"

—Rules paving a way to victory just by employing the right Word were all too favorable. Seeing what they'd missed, Sora and Shiro—no, Shiro regretted it more and bit her nails. The catch in the rules…the wording. They depended on her to remember every word so they could catch it. Shiro tormented herself as Sora rubbed her head.

"We're playing by ear here. What do you expect? Anyway, now's not the time—"

"…Mm!"

A game had been sprung on them without adequate information. It was only natural unforeseen circumstances would arise. *They'd win anyway—* How quickly they'd adapt and take control of the situation, that was the quintessence of " "— There was no time to grieve!

"—Jibril, how many of those can they fire?"

"Good question… It depends on the individual, but shall we say six or so?"

"—Well, that'll be a pain, but I guess with just six, they're not gonna waste 'em. So—"

"Oh no, Master."

Reflected in Sora's backward-facing eyes, a multitude of shadows that had gathered on the cubes—the Flügel—could be seen raising their hands…and the night sky was bathed the color of day.

"I meant that they can launch six or so at once. There is no *limit*."

"I was a fool to hope for a second that you freaks had limits!"

"…Brother, let's go—!"

This time Shiro was quicker on the trigger, flapping her wing hard. Promptly, Sora left the mini-Jibril behind in silent pursuit. The "missiles" veered toward them in complex curves—but if Jibril had been right that they were *homing*—

"...Mm!"

Shiro gave her wing a big flap. Grasping her intent from her hand in his, Sora followed suit. Even their Word of "acceleration" was insufficient to best the speed of the countless incoming rays. But the instant the beams were at their backs—a chandelle. Banking at a forty-five-degree angle from their level flight and looping diagonally upward, they revved up their speed and climbed— The "capture beams," perhaps proximity-triggered, came within a hairbreadth when the siblings' speed dipped fractionally at the start of their incline. The rays flashed behind them—and detonated.

"Hyaaaaaaaah!"

Outpacing Plum's shriek, Shiro canceled the chandelle they'd started. Instead of turning, she gave her wing one more flap, adding more speed to their ascent and breaking away from the light that exploded behind them.

—They'd survived. But allowing no time for self-congratulations, more beams pelted them, one after the other. Sora and Shiro drew them all in and flipped them off with exactly the same maneuver they'd just executed, but this time with a *sharp descent*, a slicing turn diagonally downward. Again, by the same method, they shook off the barrage that detonated at their heels and used their speed—

"Ngaaaaahyaaaaaa!"

Plum, who maintained their wings, squealed as those wings, still operating at ultra-high speeds, abruptly stopped. The barrel roll wrapped them around beams bursting at close range, one by one, as they evaded. But as the light came in wave after wave, now the siblings' wings flapped to break. On a knife's edge of control, they dove into a thin crack between cubes—and immediately— Countless explosions as beams burst around their entrance.

—Yes, homing projectiles could be guided. While the job of calculating the rays' trajectories so they could be shaken off fell to Shiro—

"...Hff...! Hff...!"

—the series of maneuvers worthy of a *Macr*ss* missile massacre gave her cold sweats and made her pant wildly. Her expression said that this was her penance for missing that no one had mentioned magic. Shiro felt weighted by that responsibility to the extent that, even after pulling this off, she looked guilty.

"—That's my Shiro. Your brother's so proud of his sister," Sora said, stroking her while cruising in a vertical orientation through the narrow passage. But—

"Aaagh, I hate thiiis! I'm done with this gaaame! If you keep this up, I'm not going to laaast!!"

How much of a load had been placed on their wings—on Plum—to support these maneuvers? It could be gleaned from Plum's wail that it was close enough to her breaking point. *Also*—Sora thought, breaking into a cold sweat of his own—once they slipped out of this crack, *without a doubt, a horde of Flügel would be waiting for them.* Considering the adaptability the Flügel had demonstrated thus far, they were unlikely to let this chance slip.

"—…Brother…I can't…"

—Yes, and this time they'd definitely be anticipating evasive action. The capture beams would surely come thick and staggered, homing in on them one after the other. Even with Shiro, there was no way they could dodge them all, and worse, Plum probably couldn't take much more. *In that case*—Sora and Shiro looked down at their wrists.

—All they had were their Words. But the only syllables they held were *roh, por, bair, vey, dih, feet,* and *teyt.* Nothing for this situation—! They cursed to themselves in their frenzy. In a matter of seconds, they'd emerge from this tight corridor. In a few moments, they'd either have to evade the imminent beams or find a Word—!

"…'*Defeat*'…! No…Brother, I'm sor—"

The first Word that popped into Shiro's head slipped out by accident, and she disavowed it in a panic.

—But, in fact, that was the Word that seemed most plausible under the circumstances. How were they supposed to defend with these syllables? Words like "evade," "armor," "reflect"—they didn't have all the syllables for any of them.

How to turn it around from here—? How to turn it around—? As Sora ground his teeth, his head spun as if it would burn up. Just seven fragments of words. All lacking application. A Word that would turn this around—turn it...around... *No.*

"—It's our job to turn...*thoughts* around, isn't it—!"

"...Huh?"

Shiro reacted quizzically to Sora's audible epiphany. That instant— different variables interlocked like gears in Sora's mind and started turning.

—Jibril's words: the capture spell triggered by proximity.

—That speed: It outstripped the Flügel, and even Sora's group couldn't shake it off.

And when he saw that light emitting—when the cogs meshed— Sora laughed.

"Why do we have to dodge—this is our chance!! Shiro, *up!"*

"Whaaaat?!"

If they flew out into the open sky, they'd be targets for the capture beams, but Plum was alone in lamenting Sora's suggestion. Shiro had a different reaction altogether:

"...Roger that!"

They'd soar up—that was her brother's conclusion. Shiro needed no more convincing than that. Maintaining their ridiculous speed, they flew up the corridor—and shot out. Sure enough—a rain of light that lit up the night rained down on them.

"Ah-wa-wa-wa-wa-wa-wa-wa-wa-waaah—yaaaaa—aaaaah!"

Nonlethal though this Flügel might have been, if they were caught, the game would be over, and their means of collecting the information they needed to determine the conditions to wake the Siren queen— For fear of these two things, Plum shrieked. But ignoring her, Sora *saw what he'd expected* and boldly cleared two syllables from his wrist to form a Word.

When the Flügel's capture beams were launched, Sora had glimpsed where the beams had originated: *the ground*. Indeed, the Flügel who had just fired the barrage that were hurtling toward them when

the siblings abandoned the corridor, without a single exception—
Every last one of them *stood with their feet planted on the cubes.*
—*The Flügel couldn't fire without landing.* Which meant—*Sora
and Shiro didn't have to dodge.* Amidst the barrage of light, Sora
grabbed the cube immediately outside their exit. Slamming the
Word he had composed into the floor—he screamed:

"—'Rotate!!'"

A moment's lag. And then, ignoring all physical laws, irresistibly,
instantly...
...*Avant Heim itself spun horizontally.*

""""Haaaaahhhhhh—?!""""

Not just Plum but all the Flügel who'd launched the capture
beams erupted in shock. No, even those above, and Jibril watching remotely, voiced their surprise. What would happen if the stage
itself were spun horizontally? Everything in the air—such as the
capture beams and the Flügel flying through them—would stay as
they were. With the Flügels' high-volume screams reverberating
in a Doppler effect, everyone on the stage (with their feet on the
ground)—namely, the Flügel snipers, Sora, and Shiro—
—would abruptly swap positions.
""""Eeeeeeeeeek!!""""
*"And the beams would be impossible to dodge by the very folks who
fired them,* descending all of a sudden before their eyes, wouldn't they?"
As Sora smiled, only Shiro could see his mouth was tense.
—To spin Avant Heim... *Unless you got it to spin on precisely the
point you imagined, it would just mean the beams would nail you
from a different direction.* His was the smile of victory born of a risky
gamble...but if the capture beams operated as Jibril described—
"Shiro!!"
Sora prodded without missing a beat, and Shiro promptly grasped
his intent and responded:

"...Syllables: *twenty-three...!*"

Yes—the capture beams were just as Jibril described.

So, if a spell that *bound its targets and pulled them back to its point of origin* activated from a reversed position—!

"Aieee!"

"Hey—wait—eeek!!"

—It would drag a gaggle of helpless Flügel right to Sora and Shiro.

"Do it, Shiro!!"

Indeed, perfectly—as Sora had wanted—they'd taken the minimum...that is to say, *only one risk.* And from the thirty-eight Flügel hauled toward them...*they would harvest twenty-three syllables: ahr, strkc, til, ah, this, uh, kuh, duhlt, luh, pit, ohn, ouhr, dis, kree, nekt, hood, mahyz, ih, min, with, skyool, kamp,* and *ree*—but.

"...B-but—Brother!"

Shiro raised an alarm.

—Trussed up in all manner of poses from their surprise, thirty-eight Flügel were delivered right to their doorstep. But *Sora and Shiro didn't know how long the binding lasted,* and the only one who knew where the syllables were was Shiro. Collecting their prizes so rapidly from twenty-three Flügel would have been too much—but Sora grinned instantly—

"First, for rating purposes! '*Vapor!!*'"

The Word "vapor" explosively covered the throng in steam. But still not finished— Breaking into a giddy leer, Sora fired off a follow-up to his Word, gesturing grandly to the audience before him (ignoring a sarcastic glare from Shiro, who knew what her brother was up to) while the siblings beat their wings hard to launch into high-speed flight—

"—And now, the moment we've been waiting for—'Baaaaare!!'"

The raiment of the awkwardly posed Flügel still immobilized by the capture beams dispersed all at once, making it possible for Sora to spot where the syllables were positioned, too. Sora, with a very *grateful* smile, closed his eyes and gave thanks.

"Ohhh, I can see now, Shiro. I can see so many *things!*"

"……Brother, take left. I'll…take right."

"Oh, entrust it to me, *my darling sister*! Yaghh, roar with thunder, O left hand of mine!"

The sister's eyes were cold enough to leave elementary particles in zero-point motion, while the brother's eyes blazed hot enough to vaporize a magnetic field.

—If temperature gradients between eyes were as effective as matters of physics, the planet would most likely have been blanketed by a typhoon.

But, fortunately—

"Uh!"

"Eek!"

—all that blanketed the area was a chorus of twenty-three moans. Sora would have liked to stay and listen a bit longer, but he and Shiro burst through it in an instant, leaving this symphony in their dust.

"—How do I put this? You work so fast… I just can't *believe* you…"

"Heh-heh-heh, please feel free to praise me unreservedly, Plum! Ee-hee-hee!"

"…Brother, you are parsec gross…"

"I just got the smack delivered in astronomical units?! Don't you know how hard your brother worked for that?!"

—Flawlessly, Sora'd plucked eleven syllables; Shiro twelve. Having also indulged in a bit of extraneous physical contact, Sora boasted loathsomely only to be bluntly chastised by his sister. Sora was obviously stung by his sister's assessment that he was approximately 3.26 light-years' worth of disgusting, but Shiro didn't stop there.

"…Brother…you wasted…three syllables…"

"Hey there, my sister, enough with your jokes. Wasted, you say? What nonsense."

With a smile so exaggerated it would make an American uncomfortable, Sora went tut-tut-tut.

"In fact, there were three noble aims behind my actions. To collect the syllables, to inhibit pursuit by provoking their reluctance to fly nude, and most important of all—"

*　*　*

Then, a beat—and with an exceedingly serious expression—
—Sora declared:
"—the will of the cosmos."
"…You mean, the will of…you…"
As Shiro corrected her brother, her voice as cold as ever, Plum shouted a warning as she noticed something closing on them from behind.
"Wahhhhhhh, they're coming at us regardless of being totally naked?!"
"…Brother, Flügel…have no shame…just, like…Jibril."
"Whaaaaat? I never expected thaaat!! …Looks like they're coming from ahead, too, huh, Shiro?"
"…No syllables."
Shiro responded with a sulk. A few nude Flügel advanced from behind, having shrugged off the capture spell. Three approaching from the front, too. Deliberately fixing his gaze on the Flügel ahead of them and promptly positioning his camera, Sora spelled a Word. As three extended their hands toward them, he and Shiro dodged gracefully—and he slammed the Word in.
"—'**Adulthood feat**'—"…that is.

At the same time, he flapped his wing to swing around, covered Shiro's eyes with the wing, and turned his camera.
"Now they should hold 'em back for us…*hff*…"
The clothed Flügel started squeezing the breasts of the nude Flügel, restraining them.
"*Hff*—at last I have succeeded in witnessing the Peach Blossom Spring with my own two eyes… It is truly marvelous. How unfortunate that it's nighttime. I wonder if my camera is getting this all right?"
"…Sir, I've almost come all the way back around to respecting youuu…"

■■■

—Endlessly lithe. Joyful. Almost as if laughing at risk, her two lords danced through the sky. Yet someone was watching this display, still showing no sign of comprehension.

"—..."

Jibril sighed for the umpteenth time at Azril, who continued to do nothing but frown.

...It looked as if her masters were going to win—but *there was no meaning in that by itself.* If Azril still failed to grasp anything, would it not betray the expectations of her masters—?!

"...Elder, why do you not understand...?"

"—..."

"Will you yet command our race to end themselves? Shall all of us die because of you alone?"

Jibril's words, smudged darkly with tension, meant nothing to Azril.

—Why should a Flügel fear death? Since when was this a feeling Flügel had? And to fear not even for her own sake—but for the others?

"Can you *see the faces of my masters, see the faces of our people,* and yet see nothing? If your thickheadedness seals away their possibilities and puts all of these six thousand years to waste—"

—Please, get it.

"They will go to waste—because of you?!"

On the verge of tears, Jibril forced out this accusation, and yet... Azril still didn't get it. Didn't get it. What was so...what was so... what was so...?!

"—......

"Nghhhh, can't catch up to them!!"

"Cut them off! We'll bring the capture spells to them by cross fire! Once they exhaust their syllables, we'll have our chance!"

"Whaaat? But they're just gonna dodge it, I'm sure!"

"We'll try it, and if it doesn't work, we'll think of something different, right? Let's go!"

As the Flügel conferred while darting about, for some reason, all of them—unconditionally, unreservedly—smiled.

—…What was so entertaining?

Anticipating the cross fire, Sora and Shiro once more flipped their wings, dropping and dodging expertly, just as predicted.

"Awww, look. I told you they'd dodge it!"

"Hee-hee! Then we'll just shoot them from above and below at the same time! Everyone disperse. Fire together on my command!"

"Yes!!"

—…What was so entertaining?! How could they chase an opponent they couldn't beat with smiles like those?

——……Seeing Azril irritated at her own inability to understand, Jibril dropped some wisdom.

"Elder. Do you remember my *spoils*?"

"……I remember everything. All the achievements of my sweet little sister."

She looked down, distantly—somewhere far in the past—and smiled.

"Nineteen joint kills of Gigants, one individual kill. Three joint kills of Dragonias, one individual kill—"

—The Dragonia head enshrined under the giant tree at the outskirts of Avant Heim had been Jibril's prize. Slaying a Dragonia alone was a feat that no one had achieved before or since. It had been Azril, in celebration, who had placed the skull—dressed it up. And—

"Three joint kills of Phantasmas—one individual kill."

Likewise, only one had ever slain a Phantasma single-handedly: Jibril. Azril's smile as she reminisced was unclouded—unaffected.

"The last created, racking up such spoils in only 245 battles, and returning home alive… How could I forget?"

…Azril recalled that faraway, nostalgic, beautiful time—*a time they had a future*—with a placid smile, prompting Jibril, not quite able to raise her eyes, to ask:

"…Then do you remember the number of times I sustained injuries sufficient to require a rite of restoration?"

"One hundred sixty."

No hesitation. Jibril had caused her worry, always returning home on the brink of death.

"...Almost all of those were instances when you *took on enemies alone*..."

A Gigant, a Dragonia, and a Phantasma—one of each. Jibril, having slain members of three higher races single-handedly, had actually been beaten back the same number of times she had been victorious—multiplied by twenty-nine. And *what that meant*...this fact being completely unfathomable to Azril...caused Jibril to grind her teeth.

"All right—do you understand why I insisted on slaying them alone?"

—Jibril's strong undertone indicated this was the final hint. Her voice was resolute, mixed with hope and the fear that hope would once more be betrayed. But...Azril could only shake her head.

"...Honestly, I never know what you're going to do, Jibs. To begin with—"

"Yes, to begin with, they were *impossible opponents*."

—Indeed, no one was supposed to be able to defeat an opponent of a higher rank without assistance. The Flügel had not been created with such abilities in mind.

—This was the end. If Azril didn't understand that—

"That is why—I proved you wrong."

———......

"...I don't get it. What are you on about? What did you see in them, Jibs?"

"......"

Jibril had no words to respond.

—That is to say, Jibril had lost all hope. The hope she'd held—that if she understood it, everyone else should be capable, too—crumbled. Her sister's despair stabbed Azril with unbearable pain. But—

"...Jibs. You're special..."

"......?"

"You don't know this, Jibs, but Lord Artosh gave you something special. That's why you can comprehend things the rest of us can't."

"......"

As Jibril stood mutely, Azril spilled out an earnest appeal.

"I want to know the Answer, too. I don't want it to end here!! Because then, what will these six thousand years have meant?! But I just don't get it—I can't go on lying any longer!!"

—Azril, the first Flügel. Created first by Artosh with the goal of perfection. *Crying* was not a feature she had been given. But perhaps because they were alone, Azril's voice, pleading, poured out for the first time with wet sincerity.

—I'm begging you, anyone, tell me.

—What are we living for?

—Why are we still alive?

—What are we looking for?

—*What do we have to find in order to have lived—?* Tell me!

Jibril listened to this silently.

—But deliberately, as if pushing Azril away in a voice without heat—

——she conveyed what Azril needed to hear...yes, *the words her masters would have chosen.*

"...And so you use your limits as an excuse—to use me."

"——!!"

"You and I, and all of us who have survived, lost, and we have lived for six thousand years as *losers.*"

Jibril turned her eyes away from Azril, hands trembling—

"That, *from this*, you have learned nothing speaks not of one possessed of an exceptional nature—but rather to your own indolence."

Jibril tightened her fists.

...Though she had nearly died any number of times, she had never been as nervous as now, she realized. She recomposed her expression: *Don't let your voice shake. Don't let your eyes wander.* She forced all the spirits that comprised her body into submission and brought them under her control.

—Could she? Doubt assailed her, but she cast it off. Do, or do not—that's what she'd *learned.* Chewing over her lessons from her masters, she *did as she had learned from them.*

—It did not come naturally to Jibril. But she decided to take a gamble—

Masters, please forgive the incompetence of your lowly servant, Jibril, on whom you have been forced to rely to the end.

So she whispered to herself, and she summoned the last of her hope—

Even so, please allow me to put my faith in the faith you have shown me.

And so with an expression that was, to the mightiest degree imaginable, contemptuous, she spat:

"*So feebleminded are you* that I...can only despise you from the bottom of my heart—you heap of trash."

For the first time in her 6,407-year life—she bluffed.

...

...—*Ff.* All color drained from Azril's face, and a tired voice rang out quietly.

"...I'm so over this."

And then—the world trembled.

⏻ CHAPTER 3 REVIEW

......I blew it.

Why hadn't she seen it coming—? Steph, accompanying Izuna out of the castle and into the surrounding town to purchase the ingredients to fulfill her promise of a scrumptious fish feast, ground her teeth at her carelessness. Fear, hateful glances, whispered threats—all of them poured down like rain on Izuna, who walked beside her. The Werebeast's senses had to notice.

"Commonwealth" or no, it cannot be so easy for people to accept another race, can it? But...

Intellectually, Steph understood. Indeed, Izuna—Werebeast—was an invader to Elkia, a subjugator. But that came from the Ten Covenants. The reason that Immanity was so taxed and tried was simply that they had lost in games. Were they to hold a grudge for a result based on mutual agreement? Was that not unjustified—?

"...Stuch, why don't you hate me, please?"

"Huh—?"

"...We took your continent, please. Obviously you should hate me, please. Because of me, they called your grampy a fool, please. Why don't you hate me, please?"

As Izuna stared at her, Steph tightened her grip on the young girl's hand. What carelessness—Steph stewed over her own lack of insight. Izuna was too clever. She'd played Sora and Shiro for the continental domain—carrying the responsibility for the futures of Immanity and Werebeast.

—It wasn't as if, in Steph's grandfather's study, Izuna hadn't read anything. She knew how her actions had affected Immanity. She'd long since grasped how she was perceived, accepting it for what it was. Only one failed to realize—

Again, it is only me...

Thinking back, when Steph had woken up—that is, after Izuna had learned Immanity—Izuna had draped a coat over Steph, a clear change in attitude. Why hadn't she realized the reason—? Steph fretted but shook her head as the young girl's eyes anxiously hovered on her. She'd been asked—so she had to answer. As they walked through town hand in hand, Izuna must have felt so much animosity. *Didn't Steph herself hate Izuna...?* This nagging concern had to be wiped clean.

Yes...I suppose. From an ordinary perspective...

Perhaps it did make sense that, if she resented the nobles who disparaged the grandfather she revered, she should also curse the Eastern Union that had brought this fate—but Steph didn't know. She didn't know why—but that was wrong. She was sure *that was wrong.* *Ff*—Steph's expression relaxed, softening.

"Why? I do not know!"

"...Stuch, are you a dumbass, please?"

"Heh-heh, perhaps I am. But—I believe *that it is wrong.*"

Steph peered into Izuna's round eyes.

—The black-haired girl, younger than Shiro, distinguished by her large ears and tail. With the weight of the world's third-largest country on her back, she'd traded blows with " " on even footing—a ball of possibility. Clever, earnest, innocent, discerning, with resolve and wisdom. Looking at this girl—Steph gave a carefree smile.

"After all, Miss Izuna, you are a good girl and adorable."

Basically, that is how it is, she thought.

"I like you, Miss Izuna. So I will give you partial treatment."

Izuna's eyes bulged. A beat later, she shook out her coat and looked away blankly. Hiding her face from Steph, she whispered weakly:

"...Stuch, you are such a dumbass, please."

—Even as she said this, Izuna slightly increased the pressure of her hand in Steph's. Steph chuckled to herself at Izuna's transparent attitude and started forward again. But then—

"Heyyy, it's Izunaaa!"

The two turned toward the cry. Several figures charged toward them, making their way through the crowd. They were young children.

"Wh-what's this—?"

While Steph stood dumbfounded, the children surrounded the two young women, and the newly assembled mob started making an awful racket.

"It's Izuna! Whoaaa, it's the real thing!"

"Heyyy, Izunaaa, let's playyy. You're super-good, right?"

"You guys are dumb. Super-dumb. Call her Madam, bighead."

"...The hell is with you assholes, please?"

Overcome by the energy of the excited children, Izuna couldn't help but respond. Steph started thinking about how to come between them. Looking closer at the boisterous juveniles, though...

...she noticed their animal ears and tails—Werebeast children. Steph addressed them in a flurry.

"What are you children doing?"

"We're playing! Togevver!"

One of the children—a girl with round ears like a raccoon dog's—answered with a babyish lisp.

"You're all...friends? Even the Werebeast children?"

"Sure we aaare."

The young round-eared girl seemed confused by Steph's dazed interrogation. Beside her, an Immanity boy raised his voice gleefully.

"*—We all became friends playing games!*"

* * *

—At these concise, simple words, Steph felt a swell of emotion that seemed to pound from deep in her heart. Meanwhile, the children gathered around Izuna romped on.

"Come on, let's playyy. I'm sooo gonna beat youuu!"

"I'm hungry as hell, please. Buying fish, please. So goddamn busy, please."

To the children grabbing at her clothes and pleading, Izuna cast a sour look—

"…I'll kick your ass next time, please."

—and then, subtly, the corners of her mouth turned upward into a grin. At these words, a particularly cheeky-looking boy stuck out his fist and cheered.

"All righhht! Remember you promised, Izuna! You can't back out now!"

"I told you, call her Madam, dumb-butts! —Madam, I am so sorry."

And so, just as they had appeared, the children departed in a tempest, waving their hands.

—Though the commotion had passed, Steph's heart pounded all the harder. That emotion was still there, like embers.

"Hee-hee… Something like this must serve as your answer, surely…"

…At some point, the feeling that poured into them from all around became one of bewilderment. Maybe it was still a little too soon. But it wouldn't be too long. By the time those children grew to be adults…surely. It would have to become a funny story that once the races were at odds— Holding this hope, Steph smiled.

"We got to play with one another— I'm sure it's more fun that way."

"…Stuch, you're not a dumbass after all, please. I think you're actually goddamn smart, please."

Hearing Izuna's offhand remark, Steph seemed struck as if in the presence of a god.

"Ohhh, Miss Izunaaa! You alone will not say I am stupiiid!"

"…But you look like a dumbass, please."

Izuna smirked a bit as Steph clung to her, weeping for joy.

—The world would change. It was changing. It kept changing. If you felt it wasn't changing, all that meant—*was you weren't looking*—

■■■

—The world was rewritten.

"Whoaaa, what the hellll?!"

Sora and Shiro, dancing through the night sky, were suddenly assaulted by a roar and a gale, shouting as they found themselves in a tailspin. But more than them—more than anyone else—Plum screeched at the manifestation of a violent whirlwind.

"Wh-what is thiiis?! So many spirits—even Flügel shouldn't be able to do thiiis?!"

A force so powerful that Plum's terrified quivering could be felt even through her scarf disguise. A force that, if viewed directly, would rob most any magic-user of sanity—incomparable, heaven-shaking—conquered the world by brute force, bent it to its will, rewrote its scenery willy-nilly...no, painted over it.

"...Uhh, Plum, is this really that bad?"

Sora's offhand question—*It's true we never prohibited stage switching, isn't it?*—was answered with a shriek.

"Bad—?! Th-this could only be an Old Deus, or, if not—"

Plum trailed off in midsentence, suddenly remembering where they were flying.

—Ixseed Rank *Two*, Phantasma—Avant Heim...

"...Don't get it. We cannot grasp it."

—Azril was static in midair. Her face now devoid of that perfect—all too perfect—angelic smile. This was not that illusion of *death* one experienced when confronted by Flügel...no. Sora let fall a drop of cold sweat and smirked. With that sort of overwhelming power—*illusion was impossible.* A force that defied perception and imagination. Sora and Shiro got goose bumps that set their skin on fire. Azril—or something that looked like her—continued slowly.

"Jibril—we cannot grasp with what sort of *fancies* they have ensnared you."

A hollow voice, absent the slightest feeling.

"—Therefore, ye shall present them to us directly."

Sora and Shiro were awestruck at this *thing* that addressed them as the scenery finally stabilized. A cracked sky stained the color of blood; dust billowing up to the stratosphere. Earth scorched beyond the horizon. The heavens were smashed, the earth was rubble, the sea was dry—dead. Innumerable fragments of shattered rock drifted around the siblings—the ruins of what had once been land. The Flügel still in the game hovered like ominous battleships in some deformed aerial fleet—

"What…what is this shit?"

Though Sora had recovered enough wherewithal to speak, neither Shiro nor Plum could respond. Only the Flügel flitting through the air seemed to acknowledge his question, wincing at that acrid sight with which they were traumatically familiar.

—Six thousand years ago—that is, toward the end of the Great War. Artosh, lord and creator of the Flügel, rolled up all their Heavenly Smites and unleashed them as a single strike of his own. A force brought down to obliterate the land, the sky, the very planet—in other words, a Godly Smite. This was the aftermath of that single blow. Framed by the twilight of the world behind her, Azril continued.

"—Erst, we fought, and we failed."

In the distant background—an enormous, ominous shadow rose up. Most likely the former visage of the land itself—the Great War form of Avant Heim. A landmass like a whale drifting through the firmament—an air fortress built not of cubes but countless artillery batteries and blue, murderous eyes.

"—Our lord unleashed his greatest strike—yet it was returned, whereupon we were annihilated, and our lord was slain."

—What was it that changed Jibril?

"Wherefore did we fail? Wherefore did we lose our lord? Wherefore did we still live? Wherefore—"

—What made us find a reason to live? Plum desperately clung to the last shreds of her sanity as the pure manifestation of violence before them demanded—

"Wherefore shall a weapon without a master live on? The answer—"

"" —'Artillery'— """

Suddenly, a flash lanced Azril's chest. A brilliant instant of illumination lit up the twilight, and a few moments later, the roar of an explosion shook the atmosphere.

"...Whng?"

Oblivious to Plum's foolish interjection—

"T—L—D—R! Finish the intro dialogue in twenty words or make it skippable!"

"...Never underestimate...the impatience...of the shmup freak..."

Sora's and Shiro's faces contorted in disgust— At some point, they'd lit upon a crag and formed a Word—and now an iron barrel protruded from their hands. Plum didn't know...hell, she'd never even seen one. Flame gushed from the 155mm howitzer the siblings had expended four syllables to materialize. Leaving sound behind, the projectile pierced Azril, and the fifteen pounds of Composition B explosive it carried detonated. An eight-thousand-meter-per-second blast blew Azril away, leaving only smoke—

"—Whaaat? What are you doiiiiing?!" Plum screamed, apparently having finally got a grip on the situation, and she gaped at Sora and Shiro.

"Skipping the cutscene."

"...Pretentious asshole...lame..."

"D-d-d-do you know who that waaas?! That was—"

"Yeah, she's Azril—and Avant Heim is the Phantasma, right?"

"...Uh, what?"

Sighing—*good grief*—Sora shook his head and said:

"Azril was the only Flügel with a horn on her head. I figured it must be something like that—but, yeah, so she's the agent plenipotentiary of Avant Heim the Phantasma or something. Well, not that I know the details."

"...Basically...Azril equals Phantasma...too..."

The two, who had digested the situation far faster than Plum, elucidated with dull disinterest.

"...Jibril said Avant Heim the Phantasma is an independent world, right?"

Sora recalled the explanation they'd been given upon their arrival.

"So the scenery changed, and that meant the world was rewritten. But, since Avant Heim is *independent*, it seems unlikely that the outside world could be rewritten to this degree. Which means—things changed within Avant Heim. But, in that case, we'd have to be *on* Avant Heim, and instead Avant Heim is in front of us—which means it's a *fantasy*."

—Proof. If she'd been real, they wouldn't have been able to harm her because of the Ten Covenants.

"...Now...Plum...here's, the question..."

Sora's and Shiro's giddy expressions, as if tickled to their cores, utterly baffled Plum as they went on.

"A large-scale stage switch, a fortress before our eyes that's like, 'Hello, I am the ultimate weapon.' And some long-ass story sequence like you'd get right before the final boss—and how much time do we have until the one-hour limit for the game is up?"

"...Nine minutes, forty-four seconds."

"What does it all add up to? We're waiting for your answer!"

—A tough question for Plum, who lacked knowledge of Sora and Shiro's old world. But: having seen everything they'd face, her brow fraught with despair, Plum, by chance—got it right.

"...The end, I suppoose?"

"What? I totally didn't think you'd get that."

Facing the massive "capture spell hell" woven of violent magic and launched from Avant Heim, Sora and Shiro once more squeezed their joined hands tightly and smiled.

"In short, this is the *final stage*—we're almost to the ending."

"...The climax... Awesome art direction...!"

They kicked off the ground and flapped their wings. Leaving behind the boom of their "acceleration," beaming, they flew into the hell storm.

"How can you *laugh* at thiiiii-eeeeee!!"

Bolting. Weaving through infinite beams, a curtain of fire launched by Avant Heim.

—The shots were incalculable, but they lacked finesse of the Flügel capture beams to home in on and retrieve a target. It was just a blanket of fire hammering away infinite rounds and speed— Ha.

"Shiro, you got the pattern figured out?"

"...Pretty much... You?"

"Come on, you know? I don't figure—I like to dodge on pure adrenaline!"

Another flap. With hair-trigger speed, Shiro matched Sora's toss of her wing. They soared headlong into the maelstrom as if dancing. Whistling, at their leisure—

"This is a yawn compared to True Hibachi Custom. Can we really count on Jibril?"

"...With a last boss like...this, we can't... The goons were...way... tougher."

Already defying Plum's comprehension with their actions, slipping gracefully through the curtain, Sora and Shiro improbably took their eyes off the barrage to check their wrists.

"—Forty-six syllables total."

"...We've collected forty..."

"We've used up twenty-three, so—"

"...We've got, seventeen..."

The syllables of light circling Sora's arm—

—*dis, nekt, min, dih, ih, ah, this, mahyz, with*—

The syllables of light circling Shiro's arm—

—kuh, skyool, pit, nuh, kree, ouhr, kamp, strik, ohn—

They had more than enough ammo. *But*—Sora noted—

"Hmmm, *cher, rey, ri, gohr, shuns, nuh*… There are still six left."

"…But our *trumps*…are in our hands."

Whereupon Shiro mumbled, *No problem, we're good.*

"—Didn't I tell you? I know the Word I wanna pound into *that* bitch. I'm short *three syllables.*"

"…Look, at this… How do you expect to…grab them…?"

Flying around in this torrent of light was already sufficient to utterly addle Plum. Taking on the Flügel on top of that was too much, even for Sora and Shiro.

"……Damn it, Shiro. Sorry, but I'm gonna use a *trump.*"

"……Brother, how many do you, need?"

"*Thirteen.*"

Atypically, Shiro's eyes grew wide, and she searched her brother's face.

"Thirteen. That's how many I need. And we're short three."

But Sora's expression—was endless sincerity itself.

—Thirteen syllables for one Word? The trump Sora spoke of—was surely a Word that could overcome any crisis. But then they could only use it once—it should really be a last resort—

"Mm, got it…"

If her brother said they needed it, that meant they needed it, no matter the risk. Shiro nodded. If she couldn't grasp the meaning behind it, her brother was right—that's all it came down to—!

—The siblings joined hands. From Sora's left wrist and Shiro's right—across their interlocked arms—three syllables dropped. And—reordering them—Sora formed a Word. He swung out his arm grandly, and then—

"**—'Disconnect'—!!**"

He slashed his arm in a grand horizontal arc—and in that moment, an invisible blade cleaved through the fusillade, through space, and even through the center of Avant Heim.

—The rule was that it would materialize one's mental image: a

Word. What one could imagine, depending on the placement of syllables—this could be adapted to any situation: attack, defense, or a combination thereof...a *trump*. Not to mention the importance and versatility of prefixes or suffixes, common sense in word games. The result of that all-powerful Word on which they had sacrificed this trump—Sora's vision.

—Everything before them, like a bad joke—was cleft in twain. The space, the scenery, the sliced *stage*: Avant Heim itself was severed—the artillery, too, was cut off.

—*And then?* Plum wondered dubiously, whereupon Sora and Shiro—*slowed down.*

"—What?!"

Plum gasped in astonishment. Amidst the crumbling scenery, the Flügel advanced through the split curtain.

"...Brother...they're coming."

"...Eighteen—more than I thought. Syllables?"

"...Six...all there...but...!"

—Right, the question was how they'd collect them. Now that they'd used "*disconnect*," they had fourteen syllables, and according to Sora, there were thirteen final syllables he had *reserved*. He'd also said he needed three of the six uncollected. Even if they succeeded in collecting the syllables, the ones they could use would only increase by three.

"—All right, time for our big, climactic gamble. Let's do it, Shiro!"

They swung around to prepare for engagement. As the Flügel bore down, they beat—well, they'd meant to beat their wings...but...

"—Wh-what?"

Plum stammered. And honestly, Sora and Shiro felt quite the same. The onrushing Flügel facing Sora and Shiro—stopped. Reverently. Yes, just like Jibril, one of the Flügel bowed.

"These syllables. You need them, don't you?"

...In time with her question, the Flügel put her hand to the *ri* on her chest. As if taking her lead, the other five syllable-bearers also laid their own bare. Sora and Shiro, bewildered, failed to fathom the meaning behind this, but the Flügel just smiled gently.

"We've already seen *all we wanted*—"

"As for the handshakes and dates and cuddle-cuddle…well, I can't say I don't care!"

"But we are quite happy just to have been able to play with you!"

"—So, if you would, please."

And then, with the words of the last—

"Please take care of Sister Azril, our soon-to-be—lords and saviors."

—Finally. Sora and Shiro got it—*the trap Jibril had planted* in the game. Feeling as if they might burst out belly laughing, the siblings reached for their tribute.

"…Ha-ha, Jibril's got her thing on now, too, hasn't she?!"

"…Jibril, for great…justice…!"

Clowning, Sora and Shiro touched the final six syllables.

"…Uh, umm, what's this abouuut?"

To Plum, the only one who didn't get it, a Flügel responded with a smile:

"Have you forgotten, worm? We, after all—"

"—Are Flügel, under the command of Sister Azril, but before that—"

"—*We are fans of King Sora and Queen Shiro*, you know?"

And so, smiling—mostly at the casual dis that cut down poor Plum behind them—Sora and Shiro chuckled to themselves and once more beat their wings and picked up speed. Toward the severed Avant Heim—and to Azril, who surely waited inside.

"…It seems some of them have understood… With this, *do you still insist that I alone am special*?" Jibril chided with a snigger.

Azril's expression—was nonexistent. But under that mask, she twisted in torment.

—What was this? What was the meaning of this? It made no sense.

Glaring at the image projected in space, Azril kept thinking. Two Immanities navigating all obstacles in the midst of a crumbling Avant Heim with divine precision. Their heading was straight—at her. As if they knew her location—! No, they *did*! By severing away the facade, they'd uncovered the scenery of old, and they'd *figured Jibril and Azril would still be in the same place*—no, they'd *concluded* it!

—In the face of this, Azril experienced a painful flashback. That's right, back then, this was how Artosh was killed. Everything was broken, everything was exposed, everything was woven through—and her lord was slain.

Wherefore we failed. Wherefore we survived! Wherefore we live?!

——......

"Wauuuhhhngyaaaaaaieeeeeeghyaaaahh!!"

"Plum! S—T—F—UUUUUU!!"

In the collapsing Avant Heim, they dashed past countless obstructions at speeds exceeding sound. One little mistake, and they'd be dead—and at the pair, who piloted this catastrophe with deranged velocity, Plum shrieked:

"Aaaaaah!! Are you two all right in the head?!"

"We are so sick of that line by now! *Shiro!!*"

Before their eyes, the scenery crumbling, countless cubes collapsed. The path was blocked. They couldn't turn—a head-on collision.

"Eeeeeeeeeeek!"

Ignoring the hysterical Plum, Shiro calmly wove a Word:

"—'Miniscule'..."

——Seventeen syllables left. With a touch of one of the cubes in front of them, the Word activated. The cube shrank, leaving a gap, but not of a size they could squeeze through...

Promptly, Sora pointed at the hole and shouted the Word he'd spun:

"—'Decamp!!'"

——Fifteen syllables left. Through the needlelike gap, it was *as if they had simply stolen past the obstacle*, and they flew on. As Plum's jaw dropped at their unbelievable adaptability, Sora suddenly asked:

"Plum, can you bare your fangs for a sec?"

"I caaan't! I don't want to 'cos I've got a bad feeliiing!!"

"Oh, really? That's too bad—I was thinking I'd give you some bloo—"

"Please excuse meee! King Sora, I'll press my fangs to your shoulder. I believe you should be able to feel theeem!!"

"—'Gore' for the win."

——Fourteen syllables left. The blood that stained his finger without a scratch soaked into Plum's fang. Plum, having succeeded in sucking blood without biting, was elated—

"Mgahhh, what eez thiiis?! This dense richness and creaaamy smoothness, this silky, soulful umami that races through my body! I can only compare it to the tears of a sea turtle laying eggs on the night of the full moon! ♥"

"You feel better?" Sora chuckled, as Plum regaled them with her incomprehensible fine dining review.

"Yeeess! I feel sooo much betterrr! I feel as if now I could do anythiiing!"

Plum—pardon, their scarf—conjured a mass of blooming flowers that soared through the air. But, at this trumpet of joy, Sora and Shiro grinned wickedly.

"…Wellll, it's nice to hear that. In that case—"

"…Let's…see you, do anything…"

"……Of course… I *knew* it would be like this. I swear…"

■■■

Six thousand years ago, Artosh had been slain. Faced with this reality they could never believe but had no choice but to accept, the Flügel had stood for six thousand years. The sword created by Artosh to exterminate gods—to eradicate other races. They had been the sword born for Artosh, to place him on the throne as the One True God. But, before the slain remains of their Lord, now no more, the matchless sword had lost its purpose. A question they had never had to consider when they had been wielded freely by the weight of command now presented itself.

—*What to do now?*

The race created by Artosh, the heralds had lost their way, and their conclusion—was to stop thinking. Whoever started it, one by one, they concentrated the totality of their power—and stabbed themselves. They were tools created to seize the throne of the One True God, and once he who would take the throne was gone, the tools were no longer needed. Faced with her sisters one after another impaling themselves, Azril—the first of them all—suddenly told a lie. No, strictly speaking, it was not a lie. But, unable to bear the sight of her sisters' suicides, the light gone from their eyes, Azril told them:

—*Our lord's mission is not complete.*

If, by some chance, improbable though it be, if thy lord should fail, be destroyed as a god of war by some unknown force...on thy lord's behalf, thou shalt unearth the cause. That remains our final mission from our lord, she told them.

—A mission assigned to Azril alone—a command. But she played it off as an order given to all Flügel and went further.

—When they had fulfilled their duty. When they had completed the last mission granted them by their lord.

—She would make the judgment as to when they were done, if they would deign to entrust it to her, she said.

...It was only stalling for time, just an expedient solution. But, even so—the Flügel began seeking out the truth behind the "unknown" that had felled their lord. As the war ended, they collected all kinds of information. As if to transform all that was unknown in the world to that which was known. And time passed, until soon it had been six thousand years—and yet the Answer had not been found. If anyone could find it, it could only be Jibril, Azril believed. The words left by their lord. The final one. *The special one.*

But.

—I'm just...tired of this...

■■■

Sora and Shiro arrived at the hall where they expected to find Azril and Jibril.

…It was dark. Sora forged a Word and activated it.

"'Ray!'"

—Thirteen syllables left. Perfect. Now, if they just slammed in that Word they were going for, they'd have beaten the game with all the syllables and achievements.

"But now we've got no more Words to use… Sorry 'bout that, Shiro."

"…If you think, it's necessary…I believe, in you."

As this line reminded him of the blessings of being a big brother—a "light" illuminated the floor.

"—For six thousand years have we sought. And yet we have not found the Answer."

On the glowing floor, an empty throne. Azril stood before it, and—

"Who the hell is *we*? I see quite a few guys other than you who have a clue."

—as he spoke, Sora saw Jibril next to her big sister, her eyes closed. Her expression was a mixture of faith and conviction, as well as—*hope for what would happen next, a quality entirely absent from Azril.*

"This vain world, this fruitless life searching for a nonexistent Answer, has grown tiresome," bemoaned Azril—and the Phantasma inside her, Avant Heim. Their true feelings as living beings—no, as *a puppet and a fantasy.*

"—If the Answer found by Jibril matches the lie we told…"

A beat. With despairing eyes deeper than hell, she focused on Sora and Shiro.

"…then we shall conclude that the reason for failure was but absurdity—and we shall end all of Flügel."

"That would be a problem."

"…Jibril's…our…d00d."

But, as the two breezily blew off this threat, Sora dove into thought: *Hmm.*

"I see. So you dipshits have been cramming your heads with books like tools to find some stupid 'Answer.' To be honest, I can't sympathize or identify whatsoever. But can I say one thing?"

And then, just as he had when first rejecting Azril's proposal—

—as if sizing up some deeply disinteresting *tool*:

"...You, *have you ever once thought up something and written it yourself—?*"

"——?!"

Azril's eyes went wide. Beside her, Jibril, whose gaze was downcast, clutched a book she called holy writ, one that had even garnered fans within Avant Heim. Written in her own hand—her observation journal of Sora and Shiro—the tale of a future yet unfinished...

"But yeah, I get it. So we were saying, if Shiro and I won, we'd get help gathering books, and if we lost, we'd be giving autographs. But you two had some bet like that going behind the scenes. We're gonna have to give Jibril a good talking-to later about betting her life without asking us, but—"

—Sora gripped Shiro's hand hard again and unfolded his wing—

"Do you seriously not get why Jibril went along with that bet?"

"—She must have been certain that you fools would present us with a convincing Ans—"

"See? You're stupid! You are so goddamn stupid!! A stupid bitch like you thinks she can act like a big sister?!"

His face descending into pure, unadulterated rage, Sora screamed:

"—She was betting on you! On her '*big sister*'! Betting her life *on her faith that you would understand*!!"

...

......

Sora and Shiro tensed their feet—and wove their final Word.

"You don't even get that, and you want her to call you 'big sister'!!"

"...Don't make us laugh... In your...dreams!"

Simultaneously—they kicked off and leaped.

—Fast. A dash employing the Word of acceleration. Sora and Shiro approached at obscene speed. But to Azril, who held within her the power of Avant Heim—they appeared motionless.

"…I see, Jibs bet her life because she believed in me…"

Even this was beyond her. She couldn't even get the point—so.

"—All right. It's time I end it all…"

Azril, too, kicked off and flew. In the hall barely a few hundred meters wide, for the two bodies moving at supersonic speeds to collide, it would take less than an instant.

—Nor was there any doubt as to the outcome. Azril would reach out, grab them, and it would be done. She hadn't found the Answer after all, *but some had*. If that was so…*it was enough*. It was time to wrap it up— *As far as she was concerned*, these six thousand years—had had no meaning at all—

"Eeyauuuugh, I'm sorry, I'm sorry! Don't kill me, pleaaase!"

…

"—Huh?"

A wail emanated from Azril's hands, which she'd closed with her eyes slightly averted. She'd thought she'd snared Sora and Shiro…but then what was this screaming in her grasp—? *Uh, what, um…*

…Hm? Did I ever hear this girl's name?

—It was some anonymous Dhampir girl.

—*Magic of illusion…* A moment too late, she got it. The Dhampirs' magic of illusion—exerted to its fullest—was capable of befuddling even Elves and Flügel. And if they'd just ingested powerful soul—blood—perhaps they could even deceive Old Dei…? But in that case, what about Sora and Shiro? Their wings—the accelerated Sora and Shiro…where'd they—?!

—As she was lost in high-speed contemplation—something whizzed by Azril at a frightening velocity. It was as if time had stopped. To Azril, everything seemed to be in slow motion. Without Plum—without the scarf—*without their wings, left only with their human selves. At inhuman speed.* Sora's fist, cocked back, tagged Azril's shoulder!

"—'Epitomize this creature with our own restrictions'—"

——No syllables left. Azril's eyes were opened. Not by the Word pounded into her. The two in high-speed flight—they'd shed their wings. Had the Dhampir cast a spell of illusion?!

"No rule that you can't use magic—amirite?"

A momentary encounter. A voice she couldn't possibly have heard— Looking back, Sora had definitely said it. But no— At that speed, as mere humans, without wings…they'd hit the ground and die in a— All this doubt and confusion was put to rest with the words that rang through Azril's ears:

"—Sixty minutes exactly… Game…over."

——No clock or anything. Shiro just read off *the timer she'd counted down in her head.* A transported Jibril softly…reverently, received her two lords.

…To Azril, it all felt so far removed, the Word worked on her. "Restrictions." The entirety of the power of Avant Heim contained within Azril was restricted. The massive power that had been rewriting space was released, and the hall around them, the scenery itself, caved in as if broken to pieces. In the center of it all, Azril went limp and stared blankly, as if to say she still *couldn't believe* it. There was no need to think back. Indeed, this was the same feeling she'd experienced when her lord Artosh was slain— Unmistakably, it was fear.

…It was beyond comprehension. She didn't understand it. She didn't understand it. There were too many things she didn't understand. It was scary. It was frightening. What was it that they understood that allowed them to walk this delicate tightrope? No matter how much knowledge you stuffed in, no matter how far ahead you planned your strategy...even if you did everything you could, at the bitter end lay the unknown—a darkness enshrouded by indeterminate variables. Amidst all this uncertainty...how? How—could they stride out onto that single, tenuous string so free of hesitation? Bearing witness to a series of events beyond all reckoning, Azril, falling, felt her consciousness drop away—

■■■

—In a dream, Azril relived her memories of her lord, Artosh.

The havoc of war, continuing endlessly, served only to fuel Artosh, god of war. An Old Deus to whom hatred, malevolence, hostility, and blood were daily bread—Artosh, lord of chaos. By this point, the fragments of his eighteen wings—the Flügel (Wings). And his messenger, Avant Heim. One god, one phantasm, and one race. This small army—was overpowering the world. The throne of the One True God belonged to Artosh—by now, no one could doubt this. This was their lord, and yet he had spoken of the possibility of defeat—just once.

"I may be defeated."

—You jest.

"I am strong."

—Of course, Lord.

"By now, there is none with power superior to mine."

—Of course, Lord.

"Therefore, there are things beyond my ken."

—Things you do not understand, Lord?

"By that which is beyond my ken, by that which the weak alone understand, by that which is unknown to me for my strength, I may be defeated."

—......

"Therefore—I shall create a being with the imperfection that, to one so mighty as me, can never be kenned."

—Imperfection, Lord?

"Can imperfection serve as perfection—can it serve transcending paradox? I know not."

—......

"However, should I succeed or should I fail—this must be the cause."

—......

"Thou who art one of my eighteen wings, the first of all, Azril."

—...Yes, Lord.

"At such time as I have been vanquished and banished from this world, thou, in the guise of the defeated, shalt take the measure of this in my stead, that I may rest in peace."

—Azril didn't know what it was that her lord saw. But the expression on her lord's face as he suggested the possibility of defeat was not fear but merely, like that of a god of war—a wish for an unknown enemy to appear...*and the drive to vanquish even that unknown*—just a vicious, but terribly amused, smile.

"Now I shall create a unit outside the series... I name her—"
And then her lord, Artosh, created what soon would become that by which he would be remembered—the Irregular Number, the Final Number...the imperfect one. The one who might look to the horizon that, in the end, even her lord could not grasp or see beyond. He called her by name.

——*Jibril*...

■■■

"...Elder. Are you awake at last?"
—Her entire body was leaden. That was Azril's first impression as she woke. Her wings wouldn't move; her body wouldn't rise— No. To begin with, her body didn't know what it meant to rise, she realized. How did you move this body? Like licking space...wasn't it? The ground—since when was it so strong, fettering her body like

this? Lifting her head that felt like a weight, Azril peered up at the shadows looming over her. Gazing down at her, Jibril—and the two Immanities, Sora and Shiro. Ixseed Rank Bottom. The weakest race looked down on her and spoke.

"So you're all 'I pwnz j00' on the strength of your cheats, and then you say the game is broken 'cos you game-over once. WTF?"

Shiro grinned as Sora laughed— But unable to grasp the meaning of his words—
"Give it another try from the beginning as a *pawn*. If you do that and still think it's broken…"
"…We'll play you…all…you want."
—Azril nevertheless understood that the Word pounded into her had *constrained her power to the level of Immanity*. She cast her eyes down and chuckled at the siblings, who smiled as they explained it to her.

—So that's how it was. She couldn't fly. She couldn't use magic. She couldn't even see spirits. Distance and weight, concepts of which she had never before been conscious, tied her body down. She rolled onto her back, worked her restricted hand, and reached up toward the sky.
—It was so high. So high, so broad. The force that held her body to the ground felt as if it had created an insurmountable wall between the earth and sky. To think she could fly out there was now beyond her imagination. Even if she were told she could fly, she wouldn't even feel like it. She didn't have the nerve. Meanwhile, those who had supposedly *played* with her, smiling and dancing through that sky though possessed of the same abilities—the two Immanities asked:
"…How's the ground taste…not bad…right?"
"After all, you don't really want to fly again until you crash once."
Having soared through those heavens with alacrity, yet saying crashing wasn't bad…

"—Come on, *when you fall, you gotta jump back up. Next round's coming, right?*"

Extending his hand with a smile—yes. As if to say, *Just as we've done.*

—At last, everything came together within Azril, and a grin spilled out. Late. Ridiculously late. Given that, she couldn't complain if they called her stupid, but Azril took his hand.

"...Elder, you are too hardheaded."

Watching with cool, yet gentle eyes as Azril stood, Jibril greeted her. The one by whom Artosh was remembered—the imperfect one. The Irregular Number, and the Final Number. Imperfection. What it meant—was the quest to be perfect. Because one was imperfect, one reached for the unknown, for the future, for hope—reached to grasp them.

—The reason Jibril had insisted on hunting alone at last—

"Jibs, you're too softheaded..."

Without even being ordered, wiping out an Elven metropolis and coming back with a grin and an armload of books. Having been told she lacked the specs, going off to slay a higher race single-handedly, and returning on the brink of death. Abandoning the Council and fleeing her homeland, then coming back with new masters— Truly, she was unquestionably imperfect and—for that reason—had *become* stronger than anyone.

"...I get it. Just reading books isn't enough to teach you anything..."

Understanding was never a matter of just memorizing facts to increase one's knowledge. It was something that came from doing, from bashing oneself, until it finally soaked into the bones. What neither Artosh nor Azril had ever been able to grasp was the "unknown." What it was—was "possibility," surely: the ability to make the impossible possible. Something that, as the strong, as ones who never failed, the ones who never lost—was beyond their ability to conceptualize. And yet—

"*Living in the guise of the defeated already made me imperfect...*I was just...scared."

It was only Jibril who had started to sense it before they tasted defeat.

—With their failure, the Flügel, and Avant Heim as well, had reached imperfection. So then...with their *pissing and whining*, it was no wonder they'd be forsaken, because of Flügel's—including Azril's—inability to do anything but collect knowledge. Only Jibril went freely where her curiosity led her to create knowledge and to leave behind what she had gained. Despite her overwhelming strength, she still aimed higher—embracing her adoration for the unknown.

—There was only one thing that could mean.

"Nya-ha, nya-ha-ha-ha...it's so *daft*. Now that I see, it's so awfully daft."

Lowering her face, Azril could only laugh now—prompting Jibril to inquire:

"I take it that now you understand?"

"...Yes, I get it—that *there was never anything to understand*."

—How could one help but laugh? To think that the answer for which they'd searched for six thousand years was—*There is no answer*...

"The unknown can never become the known, for *the known thereafter becomes the unknown*. There is no end. Yesterday's wisdom is today's folly."

Having never lost before, ever since that first defeat, Azril had feared it through and through—the unknown. The more she tried to understand it, the further it receded.

"Therefore, we shall not memorize, but learn—we shall enjoy even the risks that come with change."

And so—she could only *approach it*. Stepping out boldly—

"It was our inability to do this that lost us the War. Elder Azril, when I lost to my masters, knelt before them, and vowed to serve them, Artosh's final mission—had been fulfilled."

Her eyes still downcast—Azril whispered:

"…Lord Artosh…have I, too, finally fulfilled your last request?"

—*Can I finally stop lying?* Wiping the tears that trailed down her cheeks, Azril looked humbly to the faraway heavens. She possessed such an ability, one she'd *never known*—but perhaps, with this, he could rest in peace.

Sora broke the moment, studying her face like a peeper.

"…Hmm, I don't really get it, but you are capable of looking cute after all, huh?"

At last. For the first time, he smiled as he addressed Azril.

"…Can I ask you four questions, Immanities—? No, I mean Sora and Shiro."

—Indeed, there was no answer. She had come all the way back to the start—in which case, there was something she needed to check.

"You guys…what do you live for?"

"Shiro."

"…Brother."

"What would you do if one of you died?"

"When we die, it'll be together, so that's irrelevant."

"…What he said."

"You guys…what were you born for?"

"Dunno."

"…Yeah."

"We don't have time to think about that shit. Unlike you ladies, our life is short."

"…We're so, busy…!"

—All instantaneous answers. Sora with a smile, Shiro dead serious. But—they weren't her answers—they could only be used for reference. So, finally—Azril asked:

"Can I…be Jibs?"

"Nope. You can only be yourself."

An instant answer. Of course. Azril had known, but clouded a bit, which prompted Sora to ask—

"Well, but so what?"

Like a cloudless— (…yes, true to his name…)

"Right now, you look cute. I like you the way you are now."

—*sky*, he beamed.

...

...Nya-ha-ha.

"After searching for thousands of years, I get 'Go back to the start.' Living forever is tiring."

Yes. Those they came up with themselves...their very own— answers. She would search for herself and, like Jibril, find her own meaning.

—As long as I know...that I can...that's enough...

Azril mumbled tiredly, but then she heard Jibril apologizing to Sora.

"...Master. To have wagered my life without consulting you and still to have relied on your power to the very end...I truly cannot—"

"Ohh, about that, Jibril."

Scratching his head as if it was hard to say, Sora told her:

"This chick hasn't got the right to command all the Flügel to kill themselves—you know?"

"———————————————Pardon?"

Leaving the flabbergasted Jibril in the dust, Azril smirked.

"Oops. Did you figure it out?"

Sticking out her tongue mischievously, she gave a *Nya-nya*.

"Forbidding you from killing yourself without permission—doesn't mean I can command you to kill yourself! Hmmmmm, it's amazing no one figured it out in these six thousand years, a lie like that, nya-ha-ha-ha!"

Shiro pounded in one more nail on top of this—

"...Even, if it were the case...Jibril...belongs to us...so..."

——Having involved her masters, even preparing for death— Jibril's shoulders began to quake. But, sighing, Sora told her:

"—But *Azril could do it herself,* sure."

At his sharp tone, Jibril gasped, and Azril stopped smiling.

"From the beginning, she was only putting herself on the table. She was probably planning to kill herself no matter what. I mean, what kind of sister would ask her own little sister to die? *Jibril, isn't she the big sister you believed in?*"

The response? Silence followed by a sigh, affirming Sora's words more eloquently than anything else could have. Given that there was an Answer, and that the Flügel were capable of reaching it, even if Azril were to return the ability to commit suicide her sisters had entrusted to her, by now they probably wouldn't do it. Even if there was no answer, if, like Jibril, they could all find a reason not to die, there was no reason to expect that they'd kill themselves.

—At which point, *Azril, who had lived so that they wouldn't die,* would have seen her role end.

"…Sora, have a lot of people gotten mad at you for overstepping boundaries?"

"Ohh, yeah, they have. But the rule of this game is that no one may die. So—"

—A resounding *whap*.

"Let's play."

Sora clapped his hands and grinned.

"I mean, it sucks to dump your progress and hit 'New Game,' right?"

—So, yes, let's play.

"Then it's simple. All you gotta do is *play a different game.*"

—A game that's sure to be fun, fun, fun.

"This world—we're gonna make it way, way more fun for you."

—A game we'll never get tired of.

"You think we can do it— Come on, whatcha gonna bet on?"

…

——……

"Nya-ha… Nya-ha-ha-ha, nya-ha-ha-ha-ha-ha-ha-ha-ha-ha-ha-ha-ha-ha!!"

From her heart, for the first time in six thousand years—no, perhaps ever—she laughed spontaneously. Maybe as a consequence of having her physical performance constrained by Immanities—she laughed so hard, her stomach hurt. She laughed so hard, her eyes were getting teary, and Azril lifted her face and—

—deliberately put her arms around Sora and kissed him.

"Mmph?!"

"…?!"

"Wha—? Ma-Master?! E-Elder Azril!!"

…After several full seconds of tongue kissing, Azril moved away.

"Nya-ha-haa, there's no such thing as a game where you bet on both sides winning. ♥"

"".……""

Blowing off the gazes of the befuddled Sora and the two who glared as if to bore a lethal hole through her, Azril said:

"You *big kids*…I'm really glad you invited me to have fun with you, right when I wanted to kill myself. But still—I'm not like Jibs. I'm not worthy of being by your side—*yet*."

She waved, and turned…and walked, feeling the gravity that restricted her body. She got her little sister worrying about her; she got Immanities worrying about her; she got consoled; she even got forbidden to kill herself. After all that—she couldn't depend on them anymore. She chuckled to herself.

"—But whatever. I'll bet that you can. Until then—I'll give Jibs's faith a try, the faith in *my possibilities* she gave me. So, I hope you'll give me a little time."

■■■

"…Brother…you *got her to kiss you*."

"Hey, hold on, *she* just friggin' did it. You got eyes?"

"Master, with all due respect, the Ten Covenants make violation of rights impossible. Therefore, the fact that Elder Azril was able to lock lips with you can only mean that you permitted it, consciously or not."

"Wait, wait, wait—what kind of man would I be if I turned down a babe like that, even unconsciously!"

"…Brother, you'll take…anyone female…"

"You quite remind me of Mr. Ino."

"Hey, wait… I mean, look, I'm obviously the victim here! Come on, guys!"

Cracking a smirk at the din behind her as she walked away, Azril muttered:

"…By the way, Jibsy—"

"…It's finally Jibsy, is it? After you treated my masters so abominably, after you lied to us for thousands of years—my mild graces are beginning to reach their limit. But what is it, Elder Azril?"

Jibril shifted to big sister's side at Azril's call, remarking in ill humor. Azril dropped a *question she'd thought of herself* aloud:

"Jibsy, how do you think Immanity was able to survive the Great War?"

"……Well."

A long-standing question. A question that had tormented Jibril with special intensity recently. The standing theory was that they had been so weak that no one paid them heed, and they just *happened* to survive. But since meeting Sora and Shiro, Jibril had begun to sense something amiss. Could it just have *happened* that, as of the end of the war, *the entire continent of Lucia was the territory of Immanity*? Immanity—whence their power? Azril *thought of it herself* and expounded.

"*To lose and lose till one will lose no more*—shall we suppose that is Immanity?"

—Taking defeat and failure as a given and learning every time, not fearing the unknown, but throwing themselves into it with glee. The most imperfect race, which for that very reason thirsted more than any to be perfect—if they supposed that… Azril chuckled. Why had they survived—? No.

"…Why did we never *watch out for such a race in the War*?"

—Jibril gasped. Not just her two lords…but the old king who had laid bare the game of the Eastern Union, and Chlammy, who had collaborated with the Elves, had, together, shown her the possibilities of the race, enough to inspire awe and dread, by now intimately familiar to her. A race of people sometimes mad, giving themselves over to death itself—and yet who invariably *made it through to the next round.*

"A race that learns without end—I wonder why we never noticed such a threat?"

It meant that, no matter how frail they might be, if they kept it up forever, inevitably—at some point—they would become an inescapable threat. Had they realized the nature of such a race during the War, what would they have done? There was no need to think about it—they'd be too dangerous. They'd be wiped out on the spot.

"...And yet records of Immanity—are *nonexistent.* Wonder why?"

Yes, records of Immanity during the Great War were *completely nonexistent—unnaturally so.*

"Nya-ha-ha-ha, well, this is just something I thought of. Could it be—"

Azril looked at Sora and Shiro—

"—they *tricked us into moving all the front lines away from Lucia*?"

Yes, that sounded just like something they would do—

"And we never were able to figure out what those Ex Machinas who slew Lord Artosh were doing toward the end of the War, so—"

Smiling with all but her eyes, Azril conjectured:

"—what if *Immanity led them*—?"

What if—the death of Artosh, which sparked the end of the Great War—

—had been planned—?

"Awwww! Maybe I'm just overthinking it? Nya-ha-ha-ha-ha-ha!"

And then Azril walked off, leaving the stunned Jibril behind.

—Even though she'd thought she'd strode a good distance away, she found that she hadn't gotten anywhere. That Jibril had not witnessed her grand exit but stood calmly beside her was so funny.

"Jibsy, I'm gonna take that kid's suggestion and live with this body for a while—and also..."

—She smiled.

"...at the next assembly—I'm gonna propose that Avant Heim join the Commonwealth of Elkia."

"...I must say I still doubt it will pass."

It would be a dream for her as well, Jibril thought to herself. But Azril plied her with a huge, slimy smirk.

"We'll *observe and learn from* Elkia. We'll be a 'member in name only'...so that everyone can find the Answer we found—fulfill Lord Artosh's final mission—how's that for a pretext? Nya-ha. ♥"

Her expression implied that it wasn't for nothing she'd managed to fool them for six thousand years.

"...I must say that does sound difficult to refuse..."

To begin with, Avant Heim was a force without allegiance. It had no territory or resources. Even if they obtained formal membership, it didn't mean they'd have to help; they could simply involve themselves in the things they wanted to. And if the Alipotentiary herself said it was for Artosh—the Flügel would have no reason to refuse.

...If Azril possessed that kind of mental dexterity, then why— Jibril sighed.

"Flügel, including me, can't recognize these kids as the new lords until we all see for ourselves—that their potential is worthy of our faith. You know this, right?"

"Yes. Everyone should be aware of that. I shall continue my missionary efforts, so there is no cause for concern."

Jibril displayed her holy journal and dismissed it as a simple matter of building the fan base—ahem, faith. At this, Azril chuckled and looked back at her.

"...For now, can you personally take care of them for me, Jibsy?"

These two were a ball of the unknown. By now, Azril understood what made them so appealing. But at the same time—they were too risky. Smirking to herself that she couldn't have them dying before a conclusion was reached:

"May I ask this of you not as the Alipotentiary—but as a *friend*?"

—Jibril fell back into her usual demeanor.

"It goes without saying that I intend to protect my masters with my life—so I refuse."

"———I see...nya-ha-ha..."

Implying that *they weren't friends*—well, of course. After all she'd done, how could she presume to—?

"But if you take too long, you will miss the highlights—*elder sister.*"

—Jibril grinned as she slipped in that "sister."

...

"Don't, worry...little sister, I'll—be coming to get you, real soon."

Nya-ha-ha-ha-ha. Smiling to hold back the tears, she trotted off. After all, she'd managed to change herself in a single hour. It shouldn't take too long— Taking her leave, she stopped in her tracks, turned—and sighed. Waved.

"Hey, everybody, will someone piggyback me? And I wanna convene an assembly real quick! I need a road to my house, at least... It would be nice if someone could lay out a road for me, nya-ha-ha-ha-ha-ha!"

She strolled home, her power still sealed. Being unable to do things like fly was somehow refreshing. Filled with frivolous thoughts like this, she chuckled to herself, finding every little thing amusing. With her feet on the ground, her gaze level with theirs, her speed no greater than an ant's march, she drank in the world.

—After living for twenty-six thousand years—it wasn't so bad to try something new.

———......

—Will you accept them as your new lords?

"I'm not the one to decide that. Av'n', you should think about it yourself, too."

—...A perplexing proposal, but deemed worthy of trial.

"Well, to be honest, I do think maybe submitting to them for a bit would be all right."

—For their potential?

At this question, Azril flapped her flightless wings through the air and replied:

"Because it would be *fun*! Nya-ha-ha-ha!"

—Excitement filled her heart just thinking about what kind of game they could play next—

■■■

—Meanwhile. Elkia Royal Castle, the study of the previous king. Next to Izuna, who busied herself laying waste to a seafood spread of royal proportions, Steph skimmed a book.

Glancing at Izuna, who was devouring the food she'd prepared with true gusto, she remarked, "...Miss Izuna, you really are quite the eater."

It was so heartwarming—but then, when she remembered that Izuna's grandfather's life was on the line, she started to wonder. Izuna was desperate, too. She'd been trying, giving it her all— But, strangely—Steph could detect in her bearing no panic, no agitation, no unease.

"Ah, this is difficult to say...but, Miss Izuna, are you not worried about Mr. Ino?"

Grinding to a sharp halt—a fish still in her mouth—Izuna answered flatly:

"Hell no, please. Why would I be worried, please?"

"...Why would you...? I mean..."

"Sora and Shiro said, 'Don't worry, we'll save him,' please."

—Izuna laid it out without a speck of doubt and resumed her meal. With a sigh, Steph returned her attention to the book in her hands and grumbled. A little question had been bothering her for a while—

"How is it that you and the Shrine Maiden are able to trust those liars so much?"

It was true that they always came through in the end somehow. But the path was always too steeped in lies and fraud. How could they trust—? Steph ruminated, but Izuna came back at her with a glare.

"...Sora and Shiro aren't liars, please."

"Miss Izuna, though you have learned to read the Immanity tongue, it appears you are not yet fully proficient."

If those two weren't liars, then what were? Steph chuckled.

"They don't smell like liars—like those damn liars who smell like 'Got you, bitch.' —I hate that smell, please."

——.

Steph was at a loss for words. Izuna remembered that day when Sora said he'd save her grandfather. Sora's scent that she'd picked up at the beach—*it had put her at ease.* She gave Steph a little smile.

"Sora and Shiro smell good, please. Those assholes fool people, lead them on, tease them, please. But—*they never lie*, please—that's why I like them, please."

—Schooled by a girl of one-digit age, Steph took a breath. It was absurd, and yet it explained things—a strange comprehension flickered through her brain. Sora—that born fraud who breathed lies. How was it that even so, at times—he reminded her of her grandfather? When she thought about it, it was obvious. If he was so good at lying, then why carry himself in such a way as to always be suspected a liar?

—Why wouldn't he—*pretend to be a good person*—?

Steph noticed Izuna studying her coolly.

"...Stuch, you smell good, too, please. But sometimes you smell like a liar, please."

"H-huhh?! Wh-when did I ever lie to you?!"

"When you talk about Sora, you smell like a damn liar, please. I don't like you like that, please."

"Th-that's because Sora forced me to fall in love with him! Isn't it natural I would resist?!"

Hurt by the implication that Izuna disliked her, Steph argued with a lump in her throat, but Izuna dismissed her with a complicated expression.

"More of your shit, please... But you usually smell good, so I'll give you a pass, please."

This said, she went back to stuffing her face with fish, leaving Steph with her thoughts.

—All right, let's suppose, for the sake of argument—not that there could very well be an argument—that Sora isn't a liar. But even so—

"That doesn't justify him co-opting my feelings with the Covenants. It's complete nonsense!"

As Steph clutched her head in her outburst, a book caught her eye. On a shelf some distance away—a book with an ancient binding.

"...*The Treasure of the Prideful Princess*... A children's tale?"

A title written in Immanity—that sounded as if it belonged in a nursery. When she opened the cover, this is what was written:

—*This is a fairy tale passed down among the Dwarves*—

"A translation? The translator—isn't my grandfather, it would appear. What is this book doing...?"

Steph, mumbling, turned the page and gasped. This is what was written there.

—This is a fairy tale from far in the past. Farther than the sea—

——......

And beneath, in a familiar hand—that is, the hand of her grandfather—was a note.

—We surmise that the sleeping queen of the sea read this tale before her slumber.

—Like the princess in the tale, the queen was loved by all and possessed all.

—And thus...she desired what she knew not.

—Having everything, she craved the one thing that eluded her: a love beyond her reach—

"Eurekaaaaaaaaaaaaaaaaaaaaaaaaaaaaa!"

Izuna started as Steph sprang from her chair with a cry.

■■■

Avant Heim—a relatively large cube in the central district. This was Jibril's former dwelling, now a storeroom. She must have moved all her books and valuables to the library in Elkia, for it didn't have the feel of a living space. As might be expected of Flügel, who required no sleep, there was no bed, and there were no windows, either. The sealed room, lined with her collection of nonbook treasures, felt surprisingly comfortable to shadow-dwellers like Sora, Shiro, and Plum. As long as they were mindful of certain warnings she gave them—*Oh Master, you had better not touch those. You will probably, no, certainly die.* Spoils from the Great War, masses of skulls, and so on, but—

"…This is weird.∴"

In the center of the room rested the books which the nigh–one hundred Flügel had collected for them as sworn by the Covenants. Buried in the pile of books, dark with fatigue, Sora complained bemusedly. Shiro, on his lap, was writing something, then crossed it out angrily, groaning.

"…Masters, why do you not take a respite?"

Recognizing that the siblings were frustrated with their lack of progress, Jibril chided them softly.

—Immediately following the game, the two had dived straight into the books collected for their information. Recording her gospel, Jibril suddenly realized it had been about five days since her masters had slept—before Plum arrived. With this in mind, she urged them, but Sora scratched his head, seemingly oblivious to her.

"How is it there are nineteen accounts—and *they're all the same on the condition to wake her*?!"

"Noooo…don't tell me it was all a…waaaaste…?"

The encounter at the end of the game. The rite to deceive even Azril, who had absorbed the power of a Phantasma. Plum, exhausted from her efforts, lay sprawled on the floor, squeaking pitifully with what remained of her breath. To think she'd done all that, and it was meaningless—her expression lost all hope, but Sora pushed forward.

"The problem goes deeper than that… I'll sum up, okay?"

With a sigh, he turned to Plum.

"Siren's queen is their agent plenipotentiary. The queen bet all of her rights and then went to sleep. But for Siren, if someone wakes her up, that person would get their Race Piece, and that would be fatal—so they covered up the condition to wake the queen."

"Y-yes… That's right…"

"The ultimate way to cover something up is if *no one knows*. So they didn't tell you how you wake her up, either."

—But.

"When the current queen went to sleep, she wasn't queen yet. Siren must have tried everything they could to wake her—but that would mean *someone knew once*, but the current accounts have been *falsified*."

You following me? Sora asked, and Plum nodded.

"Eight hundred years ago, there were guys who tried to beat the queen's game. We can see nineteen of them from just the records we've dug up in Avant Heim, covering five different races, and we can see the words that were supposedly used. If we compare them, we should be able to trace them back to the condition to wake her—*or so I thought*."

Shiro moaned, *Nghhhh*, and collapsed into Sora's lap—brain fried. They'd checked the verbiage in the languages of five races, even verified the manner of the words' interpretation—but.

"'*Whosoever wakes the queen will win the queen's love and everything she has*'—that's all we can get."

Whoever wakes the queen—i.e., she didn't have to fall in love. Wins everything—i.e., you got all the rights. Those two things had been nailed down, but that was worthless by now. The real thing was—Sora griped—

"Why don't they say how you wake her—? *Is that really the part they'd leave out?*"

Before the previous queen had passed, someone getting all the rights wouldn't have impinged on the race's survival. They should have announced the victory condition to get someone to hurry up and beat it already. But then, if no such thing was recorded…

"……Worst-case scenario…"

"—Huh?"

At Shiro's dire assessment, Plum sorrowfully sought clarification.

"…*No one…ever, knew…how…*"

"…Could be that even the queen herself didn't spell out the victory conditions clearly when she made the game—for example…"

After a deeeep sigh, Sora wrung it out:

"…'Please me. Except I don't know what will please me…'—or something like that."

—Plum's eyes rolled back in her head, and she fell. Frankly, Sora felt like doing the same. If this was true, it would explain why no one had been able to wake her, why Plum hadn't been able to figure out how you wake her, why a spell that would make her fall in love unconditionally worked but still didn't wake her, and also—*how Siren had been able to cover it up completely*—everything. If no one knew from the beginning, then there was nothing to cover up. And then they'd have to attack the problem from the standpoint of "What did the queen want when she slept?"— *They were back to square one.*

"Ahh, shit, what's wrong with this bitch?!"

Oozing distress, Sora ranted and flopped onto the floor. Shiro also went GG, audibly snoring on Sora's lap, and Plum—passed out. The scene looked as if it would hang perfectly in an art museum under the title *Despair*.

"…Well, why don't I tell you a story for a change of pace."

Jibril lightly snapped her fingers, and the walls and ceiling of her house went clear as glass. As he lay sprawled on the floor, Sora saw the night unfold above him—no, that wasn't it. They floated at the edge of the stratosphere—the border between the planet and space. So it was space. This realization was accompanied by a soothing reverberation like the cry of a whale.

"…What was…?"

"It is he— 'Twas was the voice of the Avant Heim the Phantasma."

Now that she mentioned it—Sora remembered seeing a landmass like a giant whale during the game with Azril.

…The fact that he was riding on its back right now was so fantastic that it was easy to forget.

"He was once a messenger of my former lord, the Old Deus Artosh."

Jibril continued with a faraway look in her eyes.

"Artosh fell at the end of the Great War—but *he* has yet to accept this. He drifts in search of Artosh, and, when he feels the presence of an Old Deus, he approaches."

Jibril cast her gaze up—to the vermilion moon floating in the sky.

"Out there are the Elementals, Lunamana, and the Old Deus who created them."

—The giant red moon Sora had seen any number of times, either larger or closer than the moon of his old world. It was still hard to imagine that an Ixseed dwelled there.

"When the red moon is visible, Avant Heim raises his altitude at the presence of the Old Deus. However—"

With a complicated, somewhat sad smile, Jibril confessed:

"—Avant Heim *cannot reach it.*"

"…Can't reach it?"

"Avant Heim is not flying through the sky, but circling the planet—swimming along the currents of spirits invisible to Immanity. He cannot swim in space, which lacks these—and so."

Sora unconsciously followed Jibril's gaze—and was speechless.

—He'd never looked at the Milky Way with his own eyes. But a river of stars that gave the images he'd seen on the Internet a run for their money floated in the emptiness. The light flowed as if to outshine the red moon.

"He looks up at the red moon…and weeps."

The torrent of light flowed like an aurora, flickering faintly. Again, the whalelike moan he'd heard before. This time, it sounded—terribly lonesome.

"...So Phantasmas have feelings?"

—Ixseed Rank Two, Phantasma. Considering that they were listed among the Ixseeds, and that Azril had said *we*, it made perfect sense, Sora realized. But still, it was strange to think that this landmass drifting through the sky had feelings. And then—*fwoop*, it hit him, and he griped in disgust.

"...So even Avant Heim understands romantic love and I don't..."

"Pardon? Why do you suppose he understands it?"

"He feels a sense of *romance* about Artosh and *loves* him as his master—so he understands both romance and love, right?"

"............"

—Then Jibril seemed to latch onto something and asked:

"Master, is there anyone you would be lost without?"

"Shiro."

"And is there anyone you love—?"

"Shiro—ohh, so just because you understand romance and love, it's not the same thing as romantic love."

Love took different forms for each—man, this concept was a total pain in the ass. If the queen's wish when she went to sleep really did have something to do with romantic love, he was shit out of luck—Sora capitulated, but Jibril was thinking of something else.

"...I wonder if that is really how it is."

When Artosh was slain, Jibril, like the rest of the Flügel, felt loss. After that, the Flügel gathered knowledge. Searching for something without knowing what: a meaning in life, a justification for existence, a reason not to die—an answer that could never be—but Jibril found it. The answer that there was no universal answer, yet *she herself could—want to exist.*

"...? What's up, Jibril?"

It was not knowledge, but the unknown before her that made her cock her head with doubt. What if—?

"M-Master, please excuse my impertinence, but may I ask a favor of you?"

"Uh, what?"

"Could you say, 'You're useless, Jibril. I'm done with you'?"

"—…Umm, let me just point out, I have no idea what you're getting at here."

"Please. Ask nothing—humor me, if you would."

As Jibril pressed her forehead deeply to the floor, Sora reluctantly did as she asked.

"—'You're useless, Jibril. I'm done with you.' —That good?"

——.

"M-M—M-M-M—Master!!"

"—Y—y-y-y-y-y-yes?!"

A shift brought her face close enough to touch his, and Sora shrieked.

"Wh-why is it I feel much as I did the other day when you commanded me to lick the feet of that long-ear, or when I stole Lord Shiro from you in the FPS with the Eastern Union? A shuddering thrill—as if my very heart is being squeezed! Wh-wh-what is this unknown emotion?!"

"Hell if I know! But, dude, don't you have enough freaky character traits?!"

As Jibril panted, blushed, and practically drooled, Sora cringed away. But having seemingly experienced some kind of deep epiphany—Jibril nodded and announced:

"Master, for the first time in the 6,407 years since my birth—I have grasped the nature of romantic love."

"…What? Seriously?"

"Yes. At last, I shall prove my worth to you, Master. —What, then, is love?"

With this rhetorical question, Jibril knelt before Sora, hung her head, and launched into an explanation.

"Master, you have ordered little Dora to love you by the Covenants, whereupon you have systematically subjected her to the humiliation of neglect. And yet Dora herself, in whom you have planted the emotion, testifies that this is romantic love! This *unknown emotion* that occurs when my lord, to whom I have devoted myself, tells me he is finished with me—this mixture of endearment, pain, assurance, and all sorts of other thrilling feelings— This is love—!!"

"Jibril, calm down, you are getting way out of control in so many—"

As Sora muttered, now unmistakably cringing— *Wham!!* Suddenly, Shiro bounded to her feet.

"Whoagh?! Wh-what is it, Shiro? My heart almost jumped out of my chest!"

Not appearing to give a crap as to Sora's feelings on the matter:

"*...Unknown emotion...she doesn't know it...she can't reach it... she aspires to it...Azril couldn't find it...Jibril found it...Steph feels it...unknown...yet to come...hope.*"

—Perhaps eavesdropping on the conversation while feigning sleep, Shiro ticked off a series of data points and furiously scrambled through the books.

"*...The queen, who enchants everyone—... The victory conditions, haven't been———falsified.*"

Mumbling this, with a *foomp* she slammed closed the book she'd furiously extracted—and she declared:

"...Brother...I figured out...the condition...to wake the queen."

—At this simple statement, Sora, Jibril, and even Plum jumped up and stared at Shiro, who looked somehow happy— No...

"...Brother, even you...can *misread*...things."

Her smile clearly indicated utter ebullience contrasted with her usual disposition.

"...Brother, Brooother, hee-hee... Brother, you *screwed uuup*...!"

Her shoulders swayed, her feet flapped— She beamed as if gloating. Her meaning was undecipherable. Sora groaned, aghast—

"Hey—wait. What—I *misread things*? B-but reading people is my—"

"...Right. Your...specialty...but this time...I win!"

—As if giddy from the heart, Shiro boasted that, in *this game*, for the first time, she'd *out-read* her brother, and Sora felt dizzy.

*　*　*

"N-no way… If I lose at reading people, logic, and strategy, what purpose do I…?"

—" "—the two-in-one gamer who was the strongest humanity had to offer. If one of its brains could no longer read people— Ignoring Sora as he devolved into tears, Plum pressed insistently:

"Wh-what do you mean?! How can we wake the queeen?!"

Drinking in the hopes of all—and the perverse tears in Sora's eyes—

—Shiro spoke.

⏻ CHAPTER 4
REACT

"…So, that's…the deal…"

"Th-that is consistent with my grandfather's observations… Uh, is that all right?"

"My hypothesis was indeed correct. Oh, how deep is love…"

"…Really…we almost went extinct for this? …I want to cry…"

"Tee-hee-hee! ★ Heyyy, looks like your chance, Plum! ★ Amila's all excited now! ♥"

"…Sora, Soraaa, I don't get this shit one damn bit, please."

"Sorry, Izuna. I'm just a useless eighteen-year-old virgin trash loser who drags Blank down, so I don't get it, either. But you're smart, Izuna. You'll get it one day. I'm off to take out the trash."

"You're throwing yourself out, please? Then can I pick you up, please?"

"…No…Brother is mine. Anyway…Brother, get ready."

"G-get ready? O-of what am I c-capable, other than to g-get in your way…?"

*   *   *

"…There's no way…I…*can beat this game… Only…you can…*"
"Let's go, Shiro!! If you can't do it, who can do it but me?!!"

■■■

"—I'm so bored."
Unconsciously, I let out a sigh.
Oceand is the home of all Sirens. At the bottom of the deep sea, at the base of a triple-layered oceanic ridge that towers in an arc like the crescent moon. Far from the excesses of land, the sea stands pure like the walls of a castle, with no road to connect it to the outside world. Other than the nameless fish and whales, rarely is anyone allowed to visit. Clad in beautiful blue, wrapped in the protection of the water spirits, a city heaped with glittering treasures. A paradise built by the magic of the Dhampirs, brilliant with a myriad of hues.

But it is a prison.
"Ohh, isn't there anything fun?!"
Fed up with everything, I pout. The songs and dances all bore me. Of fine delicacies, I've had my fill.
Oceand. A perpetual den of pleasure. Beauty, riches, love—it's all here. Since the time I was born, all of it belonged to me. And for that reason—I can never be fulfilled. Because, out of everything, it is I who am the most beautiful, the most valuable treasure. However wonderful may be the things in this world, they can never compare to me. But suppose—somewhere—there is something that I might desire?

That would be—love! True love!
Beautiful and wonderful, an everlasting bond! The supreme treasure, which even gods must covet!
My innocent soul, defiled by no one—waits in this city of dreams for *him*. My eternal lover, who will grant me that which I do not have. The prince who will quench the thirsting of my heart. Waiting for *him*, I have slept……how long has it been?

"…—What difference does it make?"

Time means nothing insofar as *he* comes not to greet me. If my heart is not filled, my life shall remain empty forever—

—Aschente—

Now a voice comes and revives my awareness. It seems I have another visitor. These silly men who come to call on me. These adorable fools who fall before me when I grant them the slightest of smiles. I have no hopes for this man, either. True love does not come easily. But, waiting as long as I have, frustration is inevitable.

"…Well, why not? I have nothing better to do anyway. I'll go and play with him a bit."

However worthless the man may be, he should at least be good for killing time. Yes—this time, I'll be very nice to him. I'll be all smiles. I'll butter him up. I'll captivate him. And then, when the time comes, I'll jilt him mercilessly. Then maybe even that fool will come to understand—

"———love?"

"What…?"

A young man's voice falls from the sky.

"*—You want love——?*"

You want love, he asks? —Well, of course.

"…Yes, I do. Are you going to give it to me?"

"In that case—I'll give it to you!!

"You~~~~~~~~~ are~~~~~~~ shock~~~~~~~~~!!"

An impact rocks the sea. Overhead—the sky is split. I don't know how else to describe it. Cracks big enough to see from under the sea shatter the sky, and it rains down like giant pieces of glass, stabbing into the ocean—the heavens and the sea stained red as blood. Amidst the shards, the source of the voice, too, descends into the depths.

"—Here it comes~ all for love~…this guy is falling~ dowwwn~…ha."

An Immanity man with dark eyes and black hair, wearing a shirt with "I ♥ PPL" written large over his chest. Beside him, in contrast, an Immanity girl with white hair and red eyes. Both with fluttering, jet-black capes that suggest the Devil. They announce with wicked smiles:

""Pleased to make your acquaintance, Sleeping Beauty, and excuse us for disturbing your rest. We are Sora and Shiro.""

"...'Sup..."

...Hmm? Now, here's an angle. Many men have come to woo me in many scenarios, but this is the first time I've seen this approach. *But this still isn't it*— What I want is true love—not mere novelty.

"Good day, dream visitor. How nice of you to come."

That should be it. There is no man who can resist my voice—my charm—

"Oh, sorry. *We're not actually here.*"

"...*Useless, useless, useless...*"

"You're shouting into the current. No offense. Alsooo—"

The man smirks and then continues.

"You are shock~ —here I come~ *with my squad~* the sky is falling down~...yo."

Another shock. With it, the sea breaks, and at the red sky that peeps through—

"—Eeg...!"

—a strangled gasp. The sky elicits instinctive revulsion and fear, an inevitable consequence of the giant baby monsters that suddenly fill it. Through the pandemonium races one monstrous girl, a halo over her head, wings of light spreading from her hips.

"Even fools are charming when they sleep, but a fool who annoys even when sleeping—there is much to see in this world."

—Behind her, hundreds of—incarnations of slaughter, manifestations of ruin—*Flügel*...?!

"...Brother, it's not...quite...soul-crushing enough..."

"Hmm, you're right. If we wanted to perfectly reenact that horrible ending from *Drakeng*rd*, we should've brought real Flügel—but we've already sealed off Azril's power, and it seems as if they're having a lot of fuss in the Council right now. We had to resort to makeshift decorations, except for Jibril."

"Please fret not, Master. I shall make up for it by doing the work of several hundred Flügel!"

Even as the man carries on his incomprehensible conversation, he looks down at me and says:

"Come, let the game begin— *Make me fall in love.*"

.........What? Having said this, the man points to the highest tower in Oceand—to the chamber of the queen—and says:

"We're over there. If you can get there and seduce me, that will end the game."

—The heavens writhe. Countless gigantic babies fall from the crimson-stained sky. The Flügel spread their wings and fly around like symbols of death itself.

...H-he's telling me to navigate this?!

"By the way, Master—do you mind if I *eradicate the city with a single blast?*"

The Flügel fidgets as she poses this question. Meanwhile, I freeze.

"Sure, no problem. Blow away everything, *including the queen.* It'll all come back together in a few seconds. It's just a dream, after all. Jibril, you can use as much force as you want—there's no limit, so knock yourself out."

"Eh-heh, eh-hehh-guh-heh-heh-hehh, I do say, I grow excited! ♥"

—And then the two Immanities turn to me once more.

"Also, when we set up the scenario..."

"...we added your...friends, acquaintances...and family...too."

At these words, in a rush, I look around—since when were they here? *My mother, my nurse, my handmaids, even my sisters whose names I do not remember*—all wail simultaneously.

"So, you can pretty much guess how this is gonna go down..."

Smiling wryly and scratching his head:

"You and those dear to you are gonna be devoured by those falling babies, sliced up by Jibril, blown away, etc., while, you know, all kinds of shit happens to you... Yeah, I'll say it again, but, damn, that game was hard-core."

"...Brother...you got me to play it, saying it was the best game ever...and super-touching... I'll never forgive you."

"I'm sorry. It was just too traumatic for me to bear alone—but anyway."

With that, the two who call themselves Sora and Shiro speak together:

""From here on, no one will save you as you writhe to your death. Let's see how long you suffer before you succumb.""

And then—with big smiles, they say:

""DIE, MAGGOT.""

Spreading her wings at this remark, the Flügel opens her mouth.

"Now, if I may: Number One, Jibril."

The halo above her head complexly transfigures itself, becoming giant, multilayered, not unlike a magic circle. Her wings lose form as if spewing energy—and a column of light like a lance sways in her hands—

"I give my master heartfelt thanks for granting me this opportunity—

"—to use my full, unadulterated, unrestrained, unreserved power, 100 percent—Heavenly Smite— Here it is! ♥"

With only these words remaining, the world is extinguished in white.

■■■

Meanwhile—Oceand: the chamber of the queen.

"Yaaay! Miss Jib is so cooool!"

Amila raised a cheer toward the underwater projector displaying the queen's dream. Around her, a crowd of Sirens likewise cheered and danced like mad. Sprawled limp on the floor were Sora, Shiro, and Jibril, who had dived into the dream, and Plum and the Dhampirs, who had used up all their strength to transport them there and build its world. Also present were Steph, eyes rolling, and the aging Werebeast—Ino Hatsuse—to whom Izuna clung. Surveying in turn the three lying unconscious on the floor and the projector, Ino asked:

"Uh, umm…I wonder—precisely what is going on here?"

"Grampy, we came to save your ass, please. Get down and give thanks on your hands and knees, please."

As Izuna rubbed her face in the belly of her grandfather—Ino—Steph answered on the young girl's behalf:

"A lot of things happened while you were in Oceand… Yes, quite a lot of things."

—But, this not being much of an explanation, Ino just kindly held the grandchild, who clung to him as he looked on in confusion.

"…I would appreciate it if you could offer an explanation a bit less cryptic."

"Don't worry about it… I hardly understand it myself… Let me just give you a message from Sora for now."

Ahem: Steph cleared her throat.

"—'We figured out how to wake up the queen. When we told the Sirens, they got all excited and gave you back and said, "Do what you want"'…he said."

"I am afraid my comprehension is only further clouded…"

"He also said…'Relax, we're gonna wake up the queen, and we're not gonna let Siren or Dhampir go extinct. We're playing a game where we've sworn that by the Covenants. You'll see what we mean when you watch us beat the game'—and also…"

With a final titter, Steph continued.

"…'Izuna missed you, so I'll leave her here. You got a good granddaughter, Gramps'… That's it."

"Is that…so?"

Dropping a smile at the pressure of his granddaughter's nuzzling, Ino thought to himself:

—*I understand that man Sora even less than I did before.*

A cheer went up. Jibril's second Heavenly Smite had thundered. The Sirens enjoyed their celebration of it while Plum haltingly chided.

"Y-Your Highness Amila… Y-you seeee. I toootally understand where you're coming from, but perhaps some discretion would be in—"

"Whaaaat? Ohhh, Plum! You can go ahead and say it, too, you knowww!"

Amila continued with the smile of a stainless saint.

"The suffering of a stupid bitch makes everything delicious! Tee-hee-hee-hee-hee! ★"

—Her smile might have been stainless, but it was wholly absent in her eyes.

"Look, Amila even opposed cutting off her sense of pain, but, see, we are being discreet, tee-hee-hee-hee! ★"

—Indeed, it was a dream. No one and nothing was actually being harmed. On top of that, when Sora and crew had entered the queen's dream, they'd asked Plum to *block the queen's pain receptors*. This was a dream, after all. There was no discomfort. It must not be forgotten—there was purpose behind all of this, but—

"This…isn't something to take Miss Izuna to, is it?"

"Truly. Indeed, I must commend King Sora's moral sensibilities in deeming it inappropriate for children."

"…? The hell is going on, please?"

Izuna, her face still buried in Ino's belly, unable to see the display, asked in apparent curiosity. But the spectacle projected before them—Plum could only describe as:

"Hell…no, more like a *nightmaaare…*"

Indeed, it was a sight that, even without any sexual content, would unquestionably fall afoul of moral regulations.

* * *

—Even Steph had heard about it: the full power of Flügel—the Heavenly Smite. A single toss of that lance of light had vaporized the sea and turned the Oceand of the dream into a crater. But—it was a dream; everything would be mended in a few seconds. Like a small child smashing a clay sculpture, Jibril rained down further destruction. At this cycle of destruction and restoration, Jibril smiled—or perhaps more accurately, leered—and flung her arm indiscriminately. Each time, the ridge was shattered, and a trench opened up, swallowing the ocean floor.

—As if that wasn't nightmarish enough, forgetting Jibril, the fake Flügel were also blithely wreaking havoc. The baby monsters, inspiring instinctual revulsion and fear, devoured the dream's bit players. And the spectating Sirens were getting off on this hard. —It was messed up.

"...W-well, I do sympathize in a way, given the circumstances... but..."

"I-it does seem a bit excessive...speaking as one who does not know the circumstances."

Grasping the situation but not the strategy, Steph had to agree.

"...There's never been a day I didn't curse Lord Tet for setting down the Ten Covenants, buuut..."

Plum quavered with a face pale enough to faint. For the spectacle projected before them probably (no, definitely) would have qualified as a mere skirmish before the Ten Covenants—in the age of the Great War.

"Your ancestors lived through this... My deepest respects."

"...I just want to know how Immanity managed to survive this."

"Both Immanity and Werebeast had to face this... Upon our return, I must take up my studies of history once more."

Their eyes rolling back in their heads, the three onlookers were independently inspired with the same thought:

—Lord Tet, thank you for setting down the Ten Covenants.

■■■

—The first blow vaporized the sea. Laila had no choice but to crawl the parched earth. She couldn't breathe. The sun beating down on the exposed seafloor consumed her flesh. There was no pain, but her energy was sorely drained. The repeated Flügel attacks gave no respite for the sea to return. In a loop of vaporization and regeneration, the sea stripped the queen—stripped Laila—unconditionally of its protection. And then the baby monsters raining from the blood-colored sky rampaged down to devour her. There was no water. She couldn't swim. The race beloved of the sea—without the sea, even their charm—

——……

"…*Hff*… *Hff*… I—I made it…have I?"
—How many days had passed? Or had it only been minutes? Dragging her body, Laila finally arrived at the foot of the tower. Behind her the smoldering flames of hell still roared. The heavens were blanketed with laughter and the light of destruction, the earth with countless dying wails. Fear driving her to muster her strength, she opened the door and leaped through the threshold—when— She felt at her back the shock and din of the city exploding again—but Laila collapsed in relief. For inside the tower—was water. This was where Sora and Shiro were supposed to be and therefore the one place even the Flügel's attacks could not destroy, it seemed. If there was water, then she could breathe, and even charm… *At last*—she thought.
"…Hee, hee-hee-hee…hee-hee-hee-hee-hee… What nerve you have—to do this to me!"
Catching her breath, Laila, at her core—now seethed with rage.

—"Make me fall in love"?
"…That's just fine. I'll see to it that you pay the tab for making a fool of me."
With a swish of her tail, Laila ascended the water-filled tower with terrible speed.
—The queen of the sea. She who has everything. Everyone bows

before me. I can't believe you would try someone like that— I don't know what you're thinking, but—

"I hope you don't think I'm just gonna make you get down on your knees!!"

—If I can just get in one word, that will be the end.

—I'll sing a song. Make him a crawling slave. Make him lick the ground. Then cast him pathetically aside and throw him into the trench of despair. Once he gets out of the dream—my charms will convince him that reality is the true nightmare, and my rejection will make him want to die.

With a wickedly warped smile, she surged through the water as if flying—and soon, she reached the top floor...the door to the chamber of the queen... The chamber where her body should lie.

"...Make way."

—That was all. The current slammed open the door as if breaking it down.

Yes. In the sea, Laila was power. Before the volume of water spirits she possessed, everything in the ocean would kneel to her. It was a simple *law*. Nothing could defy it. It superseded even some forms of magic. Even the spirits employed in Elf rites would take Laila's side. Things she could not tame—in this world—did not exist. With unshakable confidence (no, fact!), Laila at last—arrived. Sora and Shiro—dolled up like the Devil. Sora strode forward to greet her with a theatrical, impudent grin.

"—Made it this far, have you...? Your foolishness is hilarious. However, it delights me that you are progressing—"

"...Brother, enough...of that."

"Whaaat? Shiro, how dare you skip my dialogue? I had it all ready."

While the two played out their farce, Laila faced them with eyes burning in anger. They had made a trifle of her, all right—but it was time they paid. And so the queen—Laila—formed words in a voice that would make the heavens swoon.

* * *

"NOW, ARE YOU DONE PLAYING? CRAWL BEFORE ME."

—Yes, let's start by having him crawl. Then we can take our time and entice him until his brain melts—

—However, the reply she received made Laila doubt her own ears.

"Hey, hey, were you listening? I said make me fall in love—don't you have anything sexy to say?"

—She was dumbfounded. The man and girl before her...upon hearing her voice that captivated all, regardless of sex—simply grinned back at her confrontationally.

—*Putting up a front*, Laila clicked to herself. As long as they were in the water, there could be no exceptions. Their gray matter must have already been numb with yearning. So—time to test just how long those iron masks would hold.

"...OH, YES, I'M SORRY... I GOT CARRIED AWAY AND SAID SOMETHING RUDE."

Wetting her eyes sensually, Laila spoke pleadingly.

"I WANT YOU TO LISTEN TO MY TRUE FEELINGS AND FEEL THEM—I WANT YOU. CAN YOU PLEASE GIVE ME WHAT I WANT?"

With not just her voice, but her every move—a binding force more violent than brainwashing was at work. Despite her imploring tone, it was mere input—a *command* that could not be blocked. At her irresistible, unconditional charm, Sora—trembling all over—answered her call:

"...Uughh, no thanks. I got goose bumps. Sorry, not happening."

......

——Huh?

"Look, let me just come out and say it, but you ain't my type."

———What?

"And then, under the rule that you're supposed to make me fall in love, the first thing you say is 'Crawl before me,' followed by 'I'm sorry,' and now you're saying those weren't your true feelings? I feel

like I've seen you in some meme about crazy bitches to avoid. I can't
believe hos like you really exist."

...Laila stood stunned. It wasn't a front. He really didn't feel her
charm. How was it possible—? Did they mess with the dream? No,
not even Elven magic should have been capable. It made no sense,
but one thing was for sure—this man had come with genuine conviction that he would not fall in love with her.

—Then the man looked to the girl beside him for confirmation of
something. She nodded, and he said:

"Yeahhh, I finally get to say it. 'Cos everyone always thought this
was a romance game, no one's told you before, right? I'm gonna
speak for everyone so far, including the old guy, and give you the
business, okay?"

Drawing a deep breath—Sora let it fly.

"Don't you know how old you are, sleepwalking around, prat-
tling like a goddamn moron? I mean, who the hell do you think
you are, dumbass? What? You think, 'It's only natural for everyone to be nice to me'? Even kindergartners these days are quicker
on the uptake than you, bitch! Seriously, do even know how many
years you've been asleep? Eight hundred years, bitch—eight hundred years! You think, 'Ohh, I'm, like, such a princess, waiting for
my prince for years and years'? You're over eight hundred years old,
Grandma! You wanna know how old you are? You're too friggin'
old! Sure, I love those characters with ridiculous ages, but they're
cool because they've got the brains, right?! And, anyway, you're like,
'There's no man who wouldn't fall for me'—but look at yourself,
man. It pisses me off! You call yourself a woman, then show some
grace! Sexiness only means something if it's bundled with humility!
Are you one of those? You know, the ones who think if a guy tells
them to take their clothes off, they can just drop 'em? Or one of the
others?! Those typical, so-called cosplay or glasses-porno actresses
who take off their costumes or glasses when they have sex, those
dumbasses with a romance quotient in, like, the tenth percentile at
best! If you think the more skin you show the better, then stop being

half-assed about it and just go live as a freakin' nudist! Dude, why should I even have to try to pick up some bitch I don't even like? Think about it, man—it's a waste of my goddamn time and effort! I might as well just hit on some 2-D girls! I'd get way more out of it, especially in terms of cost performance, all while protecting my heart and wallet! Oh yeah, and just let me add one more thing before I wrap up— You got these water spirits or whatever, I dunno, but something granting you charm from the shadows—but honestly, your face score is barely above average, and it's the worst among all the chicks I hang with, so would you look in a damn mirror and figure that out, you sponge-brain?!"

―――――............

Ffff... Sora, spewing this all at once with no room for argument— smiled in relief.

"*Hff*—I feel so much better... Great. I said my piece. Now I'm done with this game. Ciao!"

Huh?

"Hey, wait—!"

"Nnnope. Did you enjoy wasting your time on this unwinnable game? See ya, suckahhh!!"

With that, Sora and Shiro whisked out of existence, as if they really had ended the game. Then: The dull percussions that had been carrying on in the background stopped—

And in Laila's heart, an entirely different sound quietly resounded.

■■■

"Heh-heh-heh! Now this is *totally gonna make her snap*— That should do it, right, Shiro?"

"...Mm, Brother...for the win...exa props."

To the brother nodding in self-satisfaction, the sister raised her thumb.

—The chamber of the queen erupted in the thunderous applause from the Sirens, who had enjoyed the fine show. By contrast, there was the blanched silence of those with common sense, like Steph. Sora and Shiro had given the queen a magnificent nightmare and returned without bothering to woo her, dumping the game. Only one of them was completely baffled as to their reasoning—just one.

"*Hff*—that was most amusing... It will be a storm of envy when I tell everyone. ♥"

—Having pushed the boundaries of devastation to her heart's content in the queen's dream, Jibril's consciousness now awoke to reality. Her skin seemed to have taken on a certain luster, and probably actually had. But—those who didn't understand the purpose behind any of it (again, like Steph) cast questioning looks.

—So what was the point of all that—? Confronted with this silent entreaty, Sora assumed a grin that said: *Don't ask me!*

Sora had just done what Shiro told him to—in other words:
...*Brother, just, be...yourself.*
That summed it up.
...*Just say whatever comes to mind...to troll, the living hell out of, her...till she has, a meltdown.*

—That was all. It did hurt his feelings a bit, having his sister call that "being himself." But if Shiro said so, if his little sister was sure that was the solution, Sora had no reason to doubt it. He needed only carry out those instructions faithfully—yes, *devotedly.*

—Just then— *Crik...!* Suddenly a crack formed in the ice the queen slumbered in.

"—Huh?"

To the stupefaction of everyone assembled there—except Sora and Shiro—the crack spread. The crystal-clear ice turned stark white as the cracks spread like tendrils, and then it shattered, sending sparkling particles scattering—like stardust. As the motes of ice danced, reflecting the ambient light——the queen's eyes flitted open ever so slightly.

Before this uncanny spectacle, everyone stood speechless.

"Hey, hey! Come on, come on! Too bad the Ten Covenants won't let me hit you!! LEL, baby!!"

Everyone except Sora, who, having been given leave by Shiro to troll, wasn't about to stop.

"...I-incredible... Is it really possible for a human to be so obnoxious?!"

Paying no heed to Steph as she crossed that line of respect, the queen slowly rose from her throne.

"...Brother, that's...enough."

"Oh, really? I was really getting into it—"

With a graceful sweep of her tail—dancing, carrying herself with light ease—the queen approached Sora. A fantastic sight...yet the queen's face was red with burning—no, mild—anger as she swam to face Sora...and then:

"How I've waited for you...my prince! ♥"

Going so far as to make hearts of her eyes—she threw herself at Sora's feet.

—...

—.........

————————What?

The entire throne room was dumbstruck, but Sora, as if on guard—

"H-hey, Shiro. The hell's this? Some kind of fake-out?"

Jittery, he turned to his sister as he was suddenly overwhelmed by a sense by déjà vu...

—Of a time he had pwned someone online with a trick that was just too dirty, and they'd ended up having to hurriedly relocate as it seemed his opponent had tracked down his address and was planning to deliver a beatdown—a painful memory from his previous world. Recalling this trauma, Sora feared he might have gone too far. But Shiro casually reassured him.

"...No...this is fine...we win..."

"...Ahh, I see now."

As Shiro claimed victory, her expression contemptuous, Steph,

Plum, Jibril, and Amila finally understood. The queen—Laila—carried on making a spectacle of herself.

"Ohh, master of my heart…Please, um, insult me more! ♥"

"—H-hey, is this chick funny in the head?"

As Sora gesticulated desperately at Laila writhing at his feet, Steph remembered the meeting before the game had started and the tale she'd found in the old king's study—*The Treasure of the Prideful Princess*. Taking its conclusion into consideration—she finally grasped Shiro's *intent*.

"…Yes, it would seem so."

A tale of a beautiful princess. A princess who had everything: beauty, riches, and love. The insatiable longing of the princess for something more—*more than everything*. One man put an end to it. The princess had received all that was, from every man. Yet her desire went unquenched.

—Until the man with the *dagger*.

——A wondrous treasure beyond the princess's belief.

——*Death* moved her, and thus it ends.

—Yes, it was the tale of a princess consumed by greed and how she was slain. But the queen must have—

"It seems my grandfather identified the tale that inspired the queen to sleep, and from that…he surmised that because she had everything, she sought the one thing she lacked—*an unobtainable love*…but still."

The previous king—her grandfather—had come up with a rather poetic interpretation. Steph sighed and then looked at Shiro—the architect of the game that had just played out.

"…Yes…the queen…all loved. Had everything, so, didn't value it… That's why, she wanted this."

Finally seeming to catch up, Ino took over with a sense of deep reverence:

"I see… She wished for one with whom she could fall in love—*who would never return her affection*."

Put bluntly—or leaving it to Shiro's interpretation: Basically, she was in love with love... She wanted a love that would go unrequited. Well, that could probably be even blunter—like so:

"...*She wanted to be humiliated*...just like Steph."
"—Like who?"
Steph gaped stupidly with this query. Jibril, having come to the same conclusion, clapped her hands.
"I see. In the tale, the man who slew the princess did not seek her love—meaning that, for the princess, that man was the *one she could not possess?*"
"—What, is that the point?!"
It was Sora's voice raised in astonishment. After all, that suggested a woman who wanted what others had—that is, one who'd engage in affair after affair... Fundamentally, that made her the very definition of a dysfunctional broad, didn't it?
"What? So, in other words, if the one she loves loves her back, it kills it for her? What an annoying bitch."
"Ohhhh! ♥ Yes, I'm an annoying biiitch... I'm sorryyy! ♥"
Queen Laila, shamed and reviled, squirmed in ecstasy.
—"I shall give you all my rights"—someone should have taken more note of the implication of this. Apparently the only one who got it, Shiro verbalized the situation:
"...Brother, you have...all her rights...so be nice, and *step on her*."
"—Uh, well, okay..."
"Uh-hunhhhhh! ♥ D-do it haaarder, please! ♥"
—Plum, with her Dhampirs, up to this point had been incapable of anything but frowning.
"...And this is whyyy...we nearly perished as she slept for eight hundred yeaaars..."
Plum, having been briefed (albeit not in this much detail), sighed so deeply as to spew out her soul. But as Plum and her kin rolled their eyes, the mortified queen exclaimed:
"...What? I really was asleep for eight hundred years?"
—But—

"All you had to do to beat this game—*was kick my ass instead of falling in love with me. Are you guys stupid?*"

"The Ten Covenants say *we can't do that*! You're the stupid one, you goddamn sponge-brain!"

"Ohhhh! ♥ Yes! I am a stupid sponge-braiiin!"

—Even ignoring the Ten Covenants, Laila's charm was so overwhelming that not even Jibril or the Shrine Maiden could defy it. Failing to fall in love with Laila—a feat likely unprecedented thanks to her absolute power—was more or less impossible. Who would have suspected that she'd set just what any Siren or Dhampir would have gladly done but couldn't—that is, *bust her a good one*—as the solution all along?

"...Do you see now, Mr. Ino? Why the Sirens rejoice so?"

"...Yes, I suppose... How shall I describe this...?"

"Tee-hee-heee! ★ Sora, this show you've given us has been wooonderful, but, while you're at it, could you hit that @#$% a little harder for Amila? Yeah! Hit her so hard her head caves in!"

"Oh, I beg you, too, my master—please hit me! ♥ Hit meee! ♥"

As Amila looked up at him leering—brimming with bloodlust—and as Laila, eyes sparkling, reiterated her request...Sora asked:

"...Hey, Jibril—what is love?"

Jibril replied, smiling at her master, who was diligently averting his gaze to the ceiling:

"Is it not exactly as Miss Plum stated? *It is what you make of it.*"

Meanwhile, a short distance away, Ino was talking with Izuna, deeply moved.

"It is true; love indeed comes in many forms... Hmm. I myself am yet green around the edges."

"...Hey, Grampy. I still don't get what the hell is going on, please."

"That's very well, Izuna. One day you will understand."

But Sora sighed and wondered—*Is that really how it is?*

"...I have a feeling I'm never gonna understand."

—And with no one but the queen—Laila—satisfied, this ridiculous game, for now, came to an end...

■■■

The Kingdom of Elkia: the capital, Elkia—late at night. In the last country of Immanity, in an office in the Royal Castle, Steph, as usual, was hard up.

"...Yes, I knew this would happen. Now we have to annex Oceand, don't we?"

—Now with even more work, Steph's dark circles were permanently imprinting themselves on her face. Word was that the kingdom was also going to be incorporating Avant Heim, albeit in a ceremonial capacity. The sheaves of paper swelled higher and higher by the day, but, imagining it increasing even more, Steph turned away, not afraid—but contemplative.

"...Though this has silenced the nobles..."

—It was hard to admit, but Steph sighed at this fact as she dropped her eyes upon the paperwork. The powerful personages who had been assailing her day after day, challenging for privileges—had disappeared. Now all she was left with was this stack of procedures related to the distribution of the vast marine territory and resources Sora and Shiro had procured from Oceand—not that that wasn't enough to keep her from getting any proper sleep— But it did mark a change between Elkia and the Eastern Union...until now so imbalanced in terms of power that the concept of a commonwealth was elusive.

The seabed resources from Siren's land—waters, rather. Even from Elkia's perspective, having obtained seabed resources that even the Eastern Union could not mine, the interests they would have lost in the merger with the Eastern Union now surged anew. Dangling this bait in every direction kept things proceeding remarkably smoothly. It had been the most ridiculous game, and a conclusion at which one could only throw up one's hands—but suddenly Steph mumbled to herself.

"...Could it be that this is what they intended from the beginning—? No, that's a leap... Isn't it?"

It had all started haphazardly when Plum called on Sora and Shiro. But the final game hadn't involved the Shrine Maiden—that is, the Eastern Union—which meant *the resources from Oceand belonged to*

Elkia alone, and consequently, the power imbalance that had been the biggest obstacle to the Commonwealth had been, if far from reversed, closed enough to seem realistic. At this, Steph had to wonder...

—Above all else, they'd brought two other races under their umbrella at once. And now it appeared even Avant Heim would join them. After Werebeast—Siren, Dhampir, and then Flügel. Just as he'd boasted, Sora really had absorbed *three* other races at once. Thus he'd taken four races, without seizure of their pieces, without cost to them—no, *to their benefit*—and *brought them under his control without bloodshed.* This made Steph recall the thought she'd had when Sora and Shiro had overcome the Eastern Union—the Shrine Maiden... An idea so absurd she'd chased it from her mind, coming back to her now with a tinge of reality.

"...The Tenth of the Ten Covenants: Let's all have fun together..."
The tension in Steph's face broke—could they really do it? Could they take the Ixseeds, who had once battled to the point of reshaping the very planet, and bring them together without any killing or death—to challenge the One True God—

"...? Come to think of it..."
Steph remembered the day Sora and Shiro had bet the Immanity Piece at the embassy of the Eastern Union. One of the Race Pieces given to each of the Ixseeds, which, when collected, would constitute the right to challenge the One True God. Steph swung her gaze past the horizon. The giant chess pieces, all the more for the darkness of night, towered as if to block out the light of the moon.

—If those were the *starting pieces* of the One True God, then might it follow that each Race Piece *had its own role?* She had never seen the other Race Pieces, but the Immanity Piece that Sora and Shiro had shown them...

"...was the king...wasn't it...?"
The king. In chess—the *weakest piece.* Its importance was paramount, but everyone knew that the king's traits were even worse than the pawn's——

"For goodness' sake, clearly I am overthinking this... *Hff,* time to get back to work."

■■■

At the same time— In the courtyard of the Elkia Royal Castle stood Sora and Shiro's palace, finally completed using the architectural techniques of the Eastern Union—basically a small wooden shack. In a room floored with tatami mats according to Sora and Shiro's specifications, a clutter of countless games and books was strewn everywhere. As the siblings lay sleeping atop their futons laid out in that close space, breathing quietly—

—without sound or presence, a shadow approached. But not entirely unnoticed:

"—Yo, Plum. What do you want at this hour?"

"...You're keeping us up..."

Stifling laughs, Sora and Shiro gave up the pretense of sleep and stared into the void.

"...Ah, ah-ha-ha, ex-excuse meee... Well, you seeee..."

However had mere Immanities seen through Dhampir stealth magic? Plum canceled her spell, showed herself with an apologetic smile, and lowered her head—

"Didja come to reveal yourself?"

At Sora's query—Plum, still smiling, froze. Ignoring her reaction, Sora and Shiro sat up—grinning like children who'd just pulled off the prank of a lifetime.

"I don't flatter people. I respect you for real. You got a sweet strategy. I can't even believe—"

Sora's praise was sincere, but—

"To the very end, you managed to lead us on without telling a single lie, Plum— No..."

Ironically drawing up the corners of his mouth, Sora fixed his gaze on the Dhampir girl...no—

*   *   *

"Shall I call you *Mr.* Plum—the *last male Dhampir*?"

—*boy*, laying it all bare.

—...*Hff*. His true form discovered, the *boy who looked like a pretty girl* sat cross-legged and sighed. His troubled face was the same as ever—but his eyes, floating in the darkness, gave a hint of cunning sharper than a knife.

"...Nghh... Did I make a mistaaake? When did you figure it ouuut?"

—Huh. He really does talk like that? Sora chuckled to himself as he answered the question.

"Right at the start—I wish I could say..."

Sora glanced over at his little sister.

"Though I hate to admit it, it was Shiro who figured it out. And that was *just before we headed for the beach*."

"...V..."

Shiro threw up two fingers signifying the *V* for victory, somehow looking proud. But, grumbling with his hand on his cheek, Sora seemed severely dissatisfied.

"Which means I almost sexually harassed a dude, and I let him frickin' lick my sister's feet... God. I shoulda seen it sooner...mumble, mumble."

"Ah-ha-ha...I'm *very* grateful for that. I really *was* about to die..."

Sora clucked bitterly at the pretty boy's innocent thanks.

"—All right, how about that quiz we were doing that night on the beach— *Shall we continue?*"

"...June 20, 22:39 UTC... Plum."

As soon as he said it, Shiro began regurgitating her memory once more, as spot-on as a voice recorder.

—*Please make our queen fall in love! I've brought a plan so that you can achieve thiiis!*

Yes, this had been Plum's request on first visiting Sora and Shiro—but.

"There's one thing's that's always bugged me, and it's *this*: You didn't say 'wake up.' You only said—you brought a plan to make her *fall in love*, huh…?"

And so—

"When we were at the Shrine Maiden's, we laid two traps for you."

"…June 21, 07:28 UTC… Brother."

—*Okay, I get your sure win or whatever. But why don't you do it yourselves?*

Then Shiro continued as if to compare.

"…June 21, 07:30 UTC… Plum."

—*You see, the last male Dhampir is still youuung…*

—*It has to be at least a man with the ability to reproduuuce.*

"First of all, we kept emphasizing *sure win* over and over again, but you *never once said it was a sure win*."

"……"

"So—you must have *known from the start that making her fall in love wouldn't make us win*, huh?"

As Plum just grinned sheepishly, Sora looked back harshly. *Next*…

"Then, two… I asked why you didn't do it yourselves."

Sora frowned as if to say, there's the bit I don't like, and announced:

"I said '*yourselves*.' But you didn't say anything about yourself. You just said it had to be a guy, and brought up *some guy without specifying from whose point of view he was young*—"

Plum couldn't pull off a lie in front of a Werebeast. He could only change the subject.

"—this guy *who still didn't have the ability to reproduce* being you, right?"

Yes, based on this, the one who'd finally figured it out was Shiro. And here—

"You remember when I looked at Shiro's phone and said, 'Then it doesn't have to be Brother'?"

"…Yeeess… B-but what about thaaat?"

At the boy for whom this was apparently insufficient to tie things together, Sora scoffed.

"What was actually written there was everything I just told you."

"...!..."

"I intentionally read something different from what was written—to alert the Shrine Maiden with a lie."

Yes, Plum—the last male Dhampir—had *scrupulously avoided straight talk*. When a dangerous question arose in the form of *Is it A or B?* he'd always answer *It's not B*. But that didn't mean *Therefore it's A*, nor did it mean he was lying. For all a Werebeast was, as long as Plum stuck to the truth, she couldn't detect disingenuous sleight of tongue.

"But this leads us to some interesting implications, doesn't it?"

Sora clapped his hands—*Shall we sum up?*—and strode about the room, monologuing joyfully.

"It was *true* that you were seeking the emancipation of Dhampir. It was *true* that you could make her fall in love with your love spell. But *you knew that wouldn't wake her up*. But it had to be *true* that you were seeking your emancipation using us— Yeah, you sure give us a lot of credit. We're honored."

Shiro responded to Sora's pronouncement with a grin.

"June 20, 21:59 UTC... Plum."

—*P-p—please waiiit! Your Majesties, we have no one to turn to but youuu!*

"Yeah, no kidding. It's not like you *could* turn to anyone but us."

So. Who would Plum need for his plan—? Folks who: Could identify the conditions to awaken the queen, which even Plum didn't know. Could then awaken the queen and win all the rights of Siren just as Plum had planned. And could, if they lost, be fed without concern to the Sirens.

—They could only be of the one race the Sirens could look down on—the lowest in the ranking: Immanity. And specifically those who had Jibril's support—and by extension Avant Heim's—in particular, Sora and Shiro. But there was a problem close to Sora and Shiro: namely, Izuna and, by extension, the Shrine Maiden—the Eastern Union. Lies would be utterly ineffective against the senses of Werebeast—and therefore:

"All you could do was to pull the wool over our eyes and lead us the entire time without a single lie."

"……"

Sora clapped in earnest appreciation.

"Yeah, I'm telling ya, man, it really is an honor that you saw so much in us. To be honest, when we got to Avant Heim and couldn't use the strategy we'd planned, we were really on the spot."

"…Yeeess, well—"

The boy, scratching his cheek, apparently troubled—grinned as a wily strategist.

"If I didn't have faith in you, why would I work with you…in a game like thaaat?"

With a fearless smirk that asked, *Isn't that obvious?* the last male Dhampir tossed out the offhanded remark—which made Sora smile. Were it necessary to complete his gambit, he would throw himself into the fire. Sora had to say from his heart that the kid was a true gamer, beyond reproach.

"Still, even figuring out that much, we ended up playing right along with your plan—I mean, we didn't have any choice. I hate to say this, but seriously, good game. It's a draw, huh?"

"…Plum, props…"

Sora and Shiro sat crossed-legged and beaming.

—But…

"Ah-ha-ha, *that's where you're wrooong*—this game is all miiine!" His face still clouded, Plum looked down at them sharply.

—Just— Yes, as if licking his lips before a feast, his smile twisted.

"……What?"

—Feeling threatened by this sudden transformation, Sora braced himself. All right, they'd seen through him. But—*that wasn't enough*, Plum sneered, his expression contorting.

"What Queen Laila bet was everything she had, rememberrr? Do you still not see iiit?"

"————Wha—?!"

At these words—Sora winced and stepped back. *So you finally see it?* Plum's fiendish smirk deepened.

"Yeeess… You inherit not only her rights, but also her *dutieees.*"

"—Ah—! W-wait…but that—!"
Grasping the implication, Sora moved to shield Shiro, his eyes wide with shock. When he'd won "everything" belonging to Siren's agent plenipotentiary—it wasn't just *rights.* He'd also taken on her *duties*—in particular, the *obligation to supply Dhampir with blood!*
Plum—the beautiful boy with sharp, scintillating eyes. His troubled mien cloudless now—doing justice to the true image of the vampire.

—The *king*—the last male Dhampir suggested the status of an agent plenipotentiary, and with a wicked leer, he bared his fangs.

"Which meaaans, *wherever the chips fall*, I'll be the one *cashing in*—do you seeee? *Lesser thing.*"

"—W-wait…but that—!"
Squeaking for his life, Sora blanched with fear. Plum spread those wings suggestive of blood and exposed his scintillating fangs in a sneer.

—Its only being proper, he whispered:

"Thank you for the meaaal—!"

With that, he pressed his fangs to Sora's neck (the latter's expression a mask of horror)—

…

—tried to sink them in…and *stopped.*

"……Huh? Uh, wha…huhhh? What, whyyy?!"

…All that mystique he'd summoned vanished instantly into thin air, leaving the king of the night—as just Plum again.

"…Brother…your acting…sucks…"

"What? No, come on. This is just the part where you wanna ham it up a little, right?"

—Their terrified countenances were unceremoniously discarded. Before the befuddled Plum, the siblings sat smugly, shooting the shit.

"I'll tell you as many times as you want, Plum. That was *sweet*. And someone who can come up with a strategy that sweet—has gotta consider how he's going to free Dhampir if we do succeed in waking the queen…right?"

"___?!"

"Just like you saw a lot in us, we—saw a lot in you."

A transition then to a friendly—but gamer-like—enigmatic grin.

"*That's why* I said it. That this game—is a draw."

At these words—for the first time, Plum's eyes swelled in shock. But Sora, his mood lifted by this exchange, just spread his arms, delighted, and went on with a smile.

"Seriously awesome, d00d, I mean it! A trap set to go off automatically if we win—a *time bomb*… I've been gaming for a long time, but this is the first time I've had one dropped on me so epically!"

—Once more (with the accuracy of a recorder) Shiro spoke.

"…June 22, 01:03 UTC… Brother."

—*The queen's wager was—*'everything I have'…*amirite?*

"You *just looked down*—you didn't say yes or no. We *got that, too.*"

Sora's lead-in was ominous enough, but what followed sent sweat running down Plum's cheeks in shock—no, in abject terror.

"—So, with that! Let's give you the *booby-trap prize.*"

"…June 20, 22:20 UTC… Plum."

—*I have heard that Your Majesties intend to conquer all the races.*

This quote, merrily recited by Shiro from Sora's lap, was what Plum had said to Sora at the very beginning—

"Sorry, man. You had this wrong all along. We're *not taking anyone's piece.*"

"_____What?"

"*D00d, look*, I talked to the queen—*while you weren't around.*"

Sora squinted, as if relating a hilarious joke to a good friend.

—The punch line:

"I told her she could have everything back *except the obligation to cooperate with us*—everything including their Race Piece."

Well, she had said, *Master of my heart, please at least hold on to the right to torment me!* —a request he'd refused, Sora added wearily... Hearing all this, Plum, empty and limp, sank to the floor and sighed.

"What is thaaat...? No matter the strategy, if one goes wrong in the first steps, it's overrr..."

The more advanced the strategy, the more critical the first steps. This Plum knew well. But how could one perceive such a mistake from the jump—? The question confounded Plum.

"You just made one mistake, and it was a *careless one*. If not for that—it really would've been perfect."

"...Yeees?"

"Dhampir was weakened by the Ten Covenants. You guys knew it and even worked to account for it right away... But even so, you're still short when it comes to recognizing your own weakness. 'Cos, look, at the very end—"

Sora chuckled.

"You called us *lesser things*, didn't you? ...*That's why you lost.*"

From this statement—inferring everything, Plum sighed.

"—Ah-ha-ha... After all this, I still had pride, didn't I...? Thinking that could never happen was my mistaaake... Of all things..."

Reassuming his usual troubled expression, Plum looked up at the ceiling, muttering.

"...How could I ever think you were *really planning to challenge the One True God...*"

Hearing this, Sora and Shiro smiled with satisfaction.

—He does know. This Plum. The last Dhampir boy. He realizes. How to beat this world.

"There oughta be more d00ds like you in the world. You were this close."

"...Let's play, again, sometime...Mr. Plum..."

Watch out next time, they seemed to advise, their voices free of malice.

—*Hfff*... Plum exhaled long and sprawled onto the floor.

"Aaahh, I can't stand iiit! I thought it was perfeect... I kept my guard up against Flügel and Werebeast, and I meant to expect as much as I could from you. I did have a bad feeling in Avant Heim, buuut…"

—That chill that had flickered through his mind. His foreboding that *these two were too dangerous, had been right.*

"…*Hff*… How do you call this a draw? *This leaves nothing but the status quooo*…"

—Yes, what had changed thanks to Plum's plan? They'd woken up the queen and averted extinction, but Dhampir would continue living under Siren's tyranny. And if Siren was going to cooperate with Sora and Shiro, Dhampir could offer no defiance, given the basic principle of their symbiotic relationship.

—Amazingly, Plum's plan had been used, and they had been sucked in. In fact—indeed as had oft been repeated—*it had been accomplished in a manner that harmed no one.*

"Nghh… You win utterly and call it a drawww! Is this ironyyy?"

Plum pouted intensely at the siblings, who had so brilliantly turned his plan back on him.

"Just to point it ouuut, we're going to be slaves to Siren forever, and I am not happy with this, all righhht?"

Só—*let me just say this*, he added:

"Don't think you can lick Dhampir just like that, okayyy?"

The eyes of the king of night, capable of making all they beheld tremble, turned on Sora and Shiro— Brushing off his gaze like a gentle breeze, though, the two raised their thumbs together.

"Sure. How could we beat you if we thought you were easy pickings? Let's *game* again. We'll be waiting."

"It was fun…Mr. Plum."

—They responded with nothing but smiles lauding a kick-ass gamer. Pushed aside like a curtain, Plum—surrendered all thought and sprawled out on the floor once more.

——……

"…By the wayyy, the match is over now, righhht? I have a favor to aaask…"

Plum met Sora's eyes with the soberest expression imaginable, and—

"King Sora... Please allow me to lick your sis's feet—"

"All right! You're ready for war, huh? Let's do it! Bring it, Dhampir!!"

The slave of sweat, the perverted boy, lowered his head and shouted vehemently:

"Oh! Well then, I don't mind if it's yours, eitherrr!"

"You don't care if it's a guy or a girl? You're a drag princess, you have a sweat fetish, you'll go for either sex— Bro, that's too much!"

With a jolt and goose bumps, Sora unconsciously grabbed Shiro and took a step back.

"Now that I know how you taste, I can never be satisfied with the blood of Sireeens. This is how it iiis!"

"You say 'Don't think you can lick Dhampir' and then get on your hands and knees without a second thought? Come on, man!"

"What? No, nooo, I'll be the one doing the lickiiing..."

"That's not what I——mm?"

—Then, as if something had just occurred to him, Sora sank into deep thought before answering carefully:

"—If you're willing to make a trade, I'm not gonna let you lick Shiro, but you can lick me. After Avant Heim, why not, you know?"

"Reallyyyy?!"

"...Brother...?"

As the perverted boy chomped down on this with a flash in his eyes, Shiro still looked perplexed.

"Well, ya see, after all that, I still have no idea what love is. It seems like Shiro and everyone else got it, and I even got upstaged at the climax...... S-so—!"

Sora, descending into depression for some reason, vigorously shook his head and made his proposal to Plum.

"Cast that love spell of yours on me. Then, Shiro, can you put your hand on my chest?"

"That's no trouble at alll! Come, my preparations are compleeete. *Let's gooo!* Yeahhh!"

Plum's eyes formed a complex pattern so that he could deploy the rite at a moment's notice. But Shiro, seemingly conflicted, put her hand on her chin—and then, as if reaching some conclusion...she announced uneasily:

".......Okay...I'm down..."

"Now, as I have obtained both of Your Majesties' permissions, I shall begiiin! So, sweat, please, *hh, hh*—"

"All right, all right. I got it, so calm down..."

As they had when Plum used the spell on the Shrine Maiden—his black wings swayed and stained red. The crimson rite that crept onto his arm flowed at Sora—and just as before—with an ear-splitting sound, rouge light whirled around its target.

"*Ghh—ghh*— N-now the only thing leeeft is for Queen Shiro to place her hand on King Sora's chessst! *Let's go*, a-a-and...I-I'm about to dieee, s-so please, bodily fluiiids..."

—It seemed this really was a spell that wore him down. But as they heaved, Plum's shoulders seemed to say, *but if it's for King Sora's bodily fluids...* As he urged Shiro forward, she placed her hand on Sora's chest and said softly—

"...........Brother...I love you."

—...

——......Mm?

"...Brother... S-so...?"

Shiro asked gingerly, but Sora just looked confused.

"...So, I dunno..."

Sora looked at Shiro—yeah...it was Shiro. Just as always, a beauty without compare, his pride and joy with pure white skin and eyes like jewels, his beloved sister.

"Hey, Plum, it's *just like always*. Nothing happened. What's the problem?"

Sora asked a bit sourly, but Plum fended off his fatigue enough to answer—

"Whaaat? Th-that shouldn't—o-ohhh... So that's how it iiiis..."

And then—as if he'd figured something out, the Dhampir smirked.

"I seeee... So *that's why you let me use the spellll*? Huhh, huhhh! ♪"

"...I have no idea...what you're talking about..."

Shiro curtly averted her gaze as she replied—leaving Sora alone, out of the picture. Plum, though, seemed refreshed, the biggest riddle having been solved.

"I seee. So *that's why the queen's charm doesn't work*... Huhhh, huhhhhh! ♪"

As long as they were in this world, the siblings should have been susceptible to spirits, yet they weren't affected by the queen's charm. Under Plum's spell, Sora's definition of romantic love should have taken hold as *what he felt*, yet *his experience didn't change*. And what that meant—

"Hey, Shiro, what's the deal? ♪"

Sora was apparently a bit slow on the uptake, but Shiro looked away.

"N-now, I cast my spell juuust as I promiiised. S-sweat, pleaaase! ♪"

"...M-mghh, well, I guess I can't argue, huh?"

As Sora held out his hand, Plum pounced with a *thank youuu*.

—It seems the spell really had been cast. There was no reason for Plum to lie. But nothing had changed.

"...What does this mean? Even magic can't make me capable of falling in love? Is this the will of the cosmos?"

Though Sora griped in utter disgust, Shiro did not reply.

"Uh-hunghh! ♥ This is iiit! Ohh, it's sooo deliciouuus. What is iiit?! ♥"

Looking down at the pervert making a scene while licking the back of his hand, Sora rolled his eyes and asked:

"...Hey, Shiro... What is love?"

"...I dunno...! ♪"

Avoiding eye contact—*Shiro's cheeks reddened slightly.*

NEVER-ENDING

"…Hey, Steph. What do you think love is?"

"—Are you still going on about that? I thought you were done…"

"Apparently, I have a daughter now."

"……………What?"

…*Okay, calm down*, Steph told herself. Severely overworked as usual, Steph had been toiling in her office when Sora, Shiro, and Jibril popped by. They'd scarcely walked through the door when Sora dropped this bomb on her.

…Hmm. Interesting. Calming down didn't help at all.

"…Are you feeling all right?"

—Jibril chimed in from the side to elaborate:

"Sirens are quite fertile—and when it comes to the queen, even a few hairs from my master's head should be enough to conceive a child. You must see what a tranquil race they can be so long as the queen is awake."

Steph tried to fend off a headache:

"—No, that is not the issue… What? A daughter?"

"But, you know, even if she's my daughter, she's a Siren, so she can't leave the sea, right? That means I have to go there, but, see…I'm sort

of worrying about whether I should go... Could this be what they call fatherly love?"

—Steph had witnessed a miracle.

—It seemed a virgin had awakened to fatherly love.

"...There's no need...for you to go..."

"Hey, but this is my own daughter we're talking about!"

"To be precise, she is more of a replica of Laila, synthesized by using a minute sample of soul from your hair... But yes, that is how Sirens reproduce."

Into this fog entered Izuna.

—A large fish was clamped in her mouth—no, a Siren girl.

"...Sora, Sora, some tiny little Siren bitch came, please."

The Siren girl's first word?

"——Dad...dy...?"

—It was electrifying.

"Aaaaahh, my daughter, yes, that's right, I'm your dadgebwuhh!"

A blow from Shiro cut short Sora's mad dashing to embrace his daughter.

"Dear me. I thought Sirens were unable to leave the sea."

"That Plum bastard is here, too, please."

"Ahh...Dhampir magic, I see... But if you do not hurry and put her in water, she will die."

"Steph! Quick, get a tank! Oh, hey—there was a pond in the courtyard. Will that do?!"

"You can do whatever, but will you just do it outside?! Or will you actually do some work?!"

Surveying the raucous office, Jibril quietly considered: Here were Immanity, Flügel, Werebeast—and even Siren and Dhampir. With no sign of conflict. Even Azril—even Avant Heim—was starting to change. The world—everything—slowly but surely. Changing as it had not since the Ten Covenants—no, since even before then. Into something. Her two masters at the center—

"It seems that my gospel of my masters truly will become myth… someday not too long from now."

Nodding silently, Jibril added to her scripture—her observation journal of Sora and Shiro.

≡|ʷ||ᴣ|||||𝕀𝕀𝕀|ᵛ||| |ᴵ||ᵛ|||||К|||| —Year, Month, Day—Master experienced immaculate conception.

■■■

—The Elven Gard capital, the Nirvalen mansion.

"…I see I lose again."

Chlammy, who had been playing a game with Fiel, let out a sigh and withdrew her notepad.

"Chlammy, lately it seems you don't mind when you lose, do youuu?"

"…Of course I mind. Why do you think I'm doing this?"

Sullenly rebutting her friend's assessment, Chlammy was recording the reason for her loss. Her notes on the patterns she should have accounted for but didn't and what to do about them… In the approximate half a month since the existence Othello game with Sora, she'd already filled fifty books.

—There was no rational way for an Immanity to beat an Elf in a game with magic. In which case—she just had to uncover *an irrational way to win*. Seeing the pile of notepads that demonstrated her determination—Fiel felt a swell of pride at Chlammy's growth.

"—Oh, Chlammy, a little bird's come. Let's take a little time-ouuut."

With this, Fiel touched the gem on her forehead.

…Referring to the interception of foreign messages from the Element Linkernet as "a little bird" was quite a tasteful bit of irony. That made Chlammy smirk a bit, but the information— Fiel's eyes went wide.

"…Fi, what is it? An emergency?"

"Ah, nooo… It simply was too incredible…"

She related the news incredulously.

"Why, Mr. Sora and company have annexed Oceand—Siren and Dhampir—into the Commonwealth of Elkiaaa…"

—*Is that so surprising?* Chlammy asked, but Fiel continued—

"The Council of Eighteen Wings of Avant Heim—has also voted to join the Commonweaaalth."

—*I see. That is surprising.* Chlammy smiled. With that, on the heels of Werebeast—Siren, Dhampir, and finally even Flügel had come to Immanity. Bewildered by Sora and Shiro's frightful speed in accomplishing something most inconceivable, Chlammy said to Fiel:

"…That's a bit faster than expected. Let's hurry and pack up."

"…Why, Chlammy, you knew about thiiis?"

Are you withholding information from me? Fiel inquired sadly, but Chlammy smiled.

"It's not like that, Fi. I said *expected*, didn't I? Their strategy always adapts to circumstances."

—It was just that, if they were going to bring together all the races, sooner or later, it had to happen.

"The issue is just—it's too fast."

"…Why, I agreeee."

—Yes, too fast—if it were just about Oceand, it could be overlooked. But now that, after the Eastern Union, they were annexing Avant Heim, it became a different story. Annexing a great country and a higher race in so short a time…

—Now principal players, such as Elven Gard and Hardenfell, would be done watching coolly; they'd be on their guard. It would likely prompt them to start taking an aggressive stance toward Elkia—but this was *not a problem.*

"Just in time. It would seem that all the rush has paid off?"

"Why, rather than *rush*, I would call it a *mad scrambllle…*"

Even as she said this, Fiel gave a wry grin and packed—and with that…

"Come, Fi, let us go. I do not expect we shall be able to return for a while—"

"Hee-hee, *if they can really do it*, it will be an event so massive as to overturn the world. Why, we certainly can't miss iiit."

As they left the Nirvalen mansion behind and walked side by side down a road they would not be able to return to for a while, Fiel asked:

"Chlammy, come to think of it… What was that—'one more thing' you were saying before?"

Fiel had reached her own conclusions, but she asked anyway.

"—He doesn't lie. *To himself, ever.* That's why he can't lie."

Apparently, she'd already known. The question had been a mere formality. Fiel smiled.

—He would never be able to say, "This is the limit; this is about as far as it goes."

—For the one who had breathed life into him transcended such limits.

—To lie to himself would be to deny his sister's humanity.

Chuckling at her remembrance of this pet theory, Chlammy spoke.

"Hey, Fi, do you know the method of achieving objectives—one common to all things?"

"…Yes?"

"You guess, you predict, you get ready, you confront it—and then you fail."

"…You…fail?"

"Yes. And then you verify the reason for your failure, you fix it, you get ready, you confront it—and you fail again."

"……"

"If you do this—*an infinite number of times*, there is nothing in this world you cannot accomplish."

"…Why, that is quite the wild arguuument…"

Chlammy smirked and nodded as she watched her companion vault past being dumbfounded to being impressed.

"Yes, it is a wild argument—but I like this wild argument more than one might think."

There was nothing one could not do. What one could not do was just what *one had not done yet*—what remained was the face-off with time, But the ones who could pass down even that face-off across generations—were the weak.

"Neither I—nor Sora—is superhuman, or a genius. But there's no need to be."

It was just—

"The important thing is to try to be."

"……"

"Our infinite failures will light the path of those who follow—a lamp for walking through the darkness."

His—Shiro. Hers—Fi. Even the endless defeats of the old king, someday…must be…the lamp of Immanity, of all the races— Suddenly, Fiel asked Chlammy about the one who had influenced her so much.

"…Chlammy. In your eyes, what kind of person is Mr. Sora?"

What her question brought to mind—was the world he had seen. And so—

"He is a *person who decided to be a player.* Just a person who quit being a puppet."

And yes, one could even say—she continued—

"A person whom one day we shall surpass—perhaps?"

At Chlammy's brazen declaration, Fiel smiled and took her hand.

■■■

The Eastern Union, the capital, Kannagari—the Shrine. Under the light of the moon, a golden fox girl and a white, aging beast man—the Shrine Maiden and Ino Hatsuse faced each other. In the hands of the Shrine Maiden as she sat on the railing of the bridge over the garden pond—was the Werebeast Piece.

—While playing with the softly shining piece shaped like a *pawn* in her hand, the Shrine Maiden spoke.

"*Pureiyaa*…eh, the word has two meanings in the Immanity tongue, I'm told."

Namely—*player*—and *prayer*. One who followed their own will, marching forward—opening the unknown, confronting the future. Or one who deferred to another's will, closing their eyes—turning from the unknown, entrusting the future.

"Ino Hatsuse. To tell you the truth, 'twas my opinion that we should leave you."

There was no apology in her words. She hadn't the qualifications to give one, she said resolutely.

"Had we done that, we'd have been able to grind Dhampir and Siren into the palms of our hands with just one sacrifice and no risk."

"...Yes, Your Holiness. I understand completely."

—This was the very reason Ino did not understand that man named Sora. Why had he been saved? Ino Hatsuse had known more than well the Shrine Maiden's purpose, and he had been ready to end his days there in Oceand. And that was why he did not understand—he could not fathom that man Sora.

"—'Tis true we won that game. But we didn't need to play it."

—A ridiculous game. With a ridiculous outcome. But a game that, if fouled up, could have resulted in severe consequences for both the Eastern Union and Elkia. In the worst case—Immanity could have even sustained the kind of irreparable harm Plum had all along been plotting.

"We took an unnecessary risk. They took up the game despite this."

They most likely had some reason beyond what he had been told, Ino thought—but. The Shrine Maiden responded with laughter like ringing bells.

"...They said they made a promise to Izuna. That they'd save you."

Ino was dumbstruck. They had wagered the survival of their race for that—?

"Well, I suppose they also had their pride as gamers, not wanting to let the game default."

—But.

"To sum up, 'twas a loony game, yet Immanity went ahead and

offered themselves up as Dhampir bait. Mr. Sora and his sister did manage to turn it around on them... But to say they turned it around suggests it was known to be risky, doesn't it?"

"......"

"Ino Hatsuse, what do you make of that man Sora?"

"...To be honest, I do not know."

The Shrine Maiden intoned to Ino, whose head was bent, *I suppose you wouldn't.*

"—That man's a fraud and a swindler—but he doesn't lie. Nay, he *cannot lie.*"

—It could be, the Shrine Maiden continued.

"If he could lie to himself—then perhaps he would have become a blackguard who was easier to understand."

The Shrine Maiden knew nothing of Sora before he came to this world. Still, having had the opportunity to observe Sora and Shiro closely, she supposed they must have had trouble living. She had no evidence for this. Were she to furnish a rationale, all she could say was that it was her intuition as a Werebeast, and from experience. But—for some reason—she was sure. Why would a fellow as skilled in mind games as Sora be incapable of real-life romance—? It was that he couldn't lie to himself. Given this—he couldn't tell a woman he didn't love that he did love her. In which case—it was an interesting question why he had no attachment to his old world. But it was probably that he couldn't accept a world—that wouldn't accept *the only girl he loved.*

—That was the one thing he could never do—*even if it meant turning the whole world against him.*

"Considering all that...I think I might as well swallow my pride...Ino Hatsuse."

In the Shrine Maiden's brazen, brilliant expression—Ino saw something he had not seen for many years.

"A man who stayed true to himself, refusing to abandon you, though I would have. Are you game to give him a chance?"

Ino, to whom the question was put, lowered his head and declared reverently:

"—If it would allow *you* to once more dream. If you would show me your dreams once more."

The Shrine Maiden smiled at these words and took the Werebeast Piece—the pawn that seemed constructed of light. And flicked it into the air.

"—Mr. Sora, let's see it. The continuation of the dream I used to dream."

That *a mere piece—could fly off the board and become a player.* That, at the end of this dream she had once dreamed then let collapse—the dream would be never-ending...

⏻ AFTERWORD

—A certain day at a certain anime studio conference room. With the source material, read to a husk, in hand, the director asked the author's team at Media Factory:

"…Uhh, what's the story behind this part?"

The gazes of the original team turned as one—to focus on Kamiya, entranced with the deliciousness of the food provided. Noticing their gazes, Kamiya started to choke at the sudden question, but he held his head high and answered:

"Heh, *I have not decided!!*"

Awash in the cold rain of looks from all present, even so, Kamiya spread his arms and continued.

"If you have everything decided from the beginning, then you're stuck following that, aren't you? Do you not believe that adapting as circumstances require is the most effective and entertaining way to give readers pleasure?!"

But, to this straight-faced assertion of Kamiya's, the director grinned rather audaciously and nodded.

"So I take it *No Game No Life*—is all about bluffing?"

"That is perfectly, unqualifiedly the correct answer!! Bluffing, balls, and bullshit will get you anywhere in this world!!"

"Heh…what did you say your name was?"

"Yuu Kamiya. These munchies are delicious (*munch, munch*)."

"You're my kind of guy, 'Kamiya.' I think you will make my next drinking session a pleasure."

As the two exchanged a firm handshake signaling some common understanding, Kamiya's editor could only look on in wonder…

—This really happened. Or maybe not.

"Please don't use up a whole page on a wild fabrication."

What? The overall gist is true, right? Aren't you the one who told me to pimp the anime without mentioning any names? Well, it's true that, since I covered up everyone's personalities and manners of speech, the lines are complete fiction.

"If the lines are complete fiction, doesn't make that make the overall gist complete fiction?"

(*ignoring her*) Heh, that director…she's something. All the reference materials she gets out are total balls-out bullshit, going way beyond anything I imagined. Though if you tell me to draw *that* shit in the comic, I'll be running away at 64 FPS.

—So, Editor S (or shall I call you Ms. Fishboard after your entry into Media Factory for your love of fish cake boards?)…you mentioned that I should casually promote the anime. Is this about what you're looking for?

"(*smiling*) Except for the fact that it's not casual in the slightest, I suppose it's fine."

All right, then… Nice to see you again. It's Yuu Kamiya. I am quite relieved to see that by some miracle, Volume 5 is coming out without a hitch.

"I should say so, after what you did to our deadlines, as usual."

Oh, about that—there's a startling fact I wanted to share with you. Did you know that humans are incapable of doing novels, illustrations, comics, and conferences at the same time?

"Well, yes. Doesn't that go without saying?"

Hmm, then, with that in mind, please look over my schedule here.

—How about it? Do you notice anything strange?

"I see various tasks related to novels, illustrations, comics, and anime all smashed up together. What about it?"

......

Dear readers, I imagine you will have understood for yourselves. But the true wonder of this matter is that Volume 5 has made it to print.

"Goodness, there is much in this world beyond the realm of human knowledge."

Yes, I am leading a fulfilling life, overturning all kinds of existing knowledge day by day (*rolls eyes*).

—So, how did you like *No Game No Life*, Volume 5? Now there is also an anime under way, and in addition, Volume 1 of *No Game No Life: The Comic*, a joint project of Yuu Kamiya and Mashiro Hiiragi, is going on shelves at the same time, so I earnestly hope you will take a look at that, too, and discover both forms to your liking. Finally, I'd like to take this opportunity to extend my deep thanks to everyone involved, *except Ms. Fishboard*.

"Huh, why everyone except for me?!"

Look at this. This crazed e-mail insisting that I get in the manuscript for Volume 6 by the end of the year.

"Whaat? Mr. Kamiya, I know you can do it; it's not like you to give u

THE OLDEST MYTH THAT LED TO THE NEWEST— THE STORY OF THE BEGINNING, THE FIRST TWO WHO SHOWED WHAT PUREIYAA SHOULD STAND FOR IN THIS WORLD—

NO GAME NO LIFE, VOL. 6 IN PRODUCTION, AS MY EDITOR DEMANDS THAT I HAND IT OVER NOW!

THE GREAT WAR THAT SPLIT THE HEAVENS, RENT THE EARTH, AND MURDERED THE PLANET... AN IMMANITY MAN WHO HELD THAT SUCH A WORLD WAS A "GAME," AND THE EX MACHINA GIRL WHO TOOK HIS SIDE—

FACTS OF HISTORY, LEFT IN NO MEMORIES AND NO RECORDS, WHICH COULD NEVER BECOME LEGEND, YET A MYTH THAT I ALONE WILL NEVER FORGET...